1. 00

D0728251

Allyson

by

Jerry B. Jenkins

MOODY PRESS

CHICAGO

©1981 by
JERRY B. JENKINS

All rights reserved

Library of Congress Cataloging in Publication Data
Jenkins, Jerry B.
Allyson.
I. Title.
PS3560.E485A79   813'.54   81-9665
ISBN 0-8024-4315-X   AACR2

3 4 5 6 7 Printing/LC/Year 87 86 85 84 83

Printed in the United States of America

To Kent Puckett,
whose friendship is a treasure

Chapter One

. I was surprised when Allyson Scheel entered our side of the building, but I confess it wasn't the first time I had watched her return from lunch. And I wasn't the only one. Even the two women in our office—my fiancée, Margo, and Bonnie, our receptionist—had caught themselves staring more than once.

It wasn't anything strange. Allyson, whom we guessed to be about twenty-five, was just one of those people who knew how to dress, how to carry herself, how to walk purposefully yet without conceit. She looked like somebody. She *was* somebody. And her long red hair and appropriately pink complexion didn't hurt, either.

Allyson and her mother, Mrs. Beatrice Scheel, owned the boutique on the first floor of the building, so we were on enough of a nod and smile basis that I knew when and where she usually lunched, and I just happened to be gazing out our second-floor window frequently at 12:30 P.M.

Margo wasn't jealous. I had tagged along once when she visited the Beatrice Boutique, and she had commented on Allyson's striking appearance. "I wouldn't

9

even call it sexy, would you, Philip? More dynamic, classy.''

"Yeah," I had said, watching Allyson move from behind the counter to the little office where her mother sat behind a desk. I got the impression that neither Allyson nor her mother personally waited on new customers.

That little visit had taught Margo and me a few things about Beatrice Boutique, too. Margo tried on a couple of dresses and then asked the salesgirl, "How much is this one?"

"Excuse me?" the girl had said.

"How much?"

The girl betrayed a flash of condescension and tried to hide her surprise. "You mean you'd like to know the price?"

Undaunted, Margo said, "Yes, I'd like to know the price.''

"One moment. I'll check."

By the time the girl returned with the news that the dress was about a hundred dollars more than Margo had in mind, we had figured that a boutique without price tags, where customers were expected to sign for what they wanted and pay whatever total arose, was slightly out of our class.

Still, the young co-owner was fun to look at. And now here she came, entering our side of the building.

I was peering down from close to the window—to see if maybe I was mistaken and she was just heading to the drugstore or somewhere—when I heard her trotting up the stairs. I wheeled around so it wouldn't be too obvious that I had been ogling her every step. Our huge outer office and double glass doors were between her and me, and with Bonnie at lunch, I was supposed to be watching the phone and the door. I hurried out of my office just as she stopped at the top of the stairs to read our sign: "EH Detective Agency/Private Investigations."

It would have been classier, I know, to have let her decide if she was at the right place, but I had momentum, after all. I pushed the door open to ask if I could help her and almost knocked her back down the stairs.

As I gushed apologies, somehow blurting her name in the process, she smiled forgivingly. "How do you know my name?" she asked.

"Oh, well, you know, we're detectives and all, ha, ha."

She raised one eyebrow to indicate that her question still needed an answer.

"No, seriously, we, uh, I, uh, well, you know Earl, Earl Haymeyer, my boss, owns this building, and even though he has a firm that maintains it and collects the rent and everything, he's still the landlord, and he knows you, I mean, he knows, ya know, that your mother and you own the boutique there."

I sat in Bonnie's chair at the switchboard and gestured to a visitor's chair for Allyson.

"So Earl, your boss and my landlord, talks about me?" She appeared slightly amused.

"Oh, no, no, it's just that we see you around, ya

11

know. We figure Earl knows the regulars, so we asked, or at least Ship asked. Larry Shipman—he's one of our men. Well, he's our only man 'sides Earl and me. We're a small shop here. Private investigations."

"So your sign says."

"Right."

"Right," she said.

Allyson looked expectantly at me, and I didn't know if she expected me to whip out a menu of what we charged for various kinds of cases or what. The phone bought me time. It was Margo calling from the deli down the street. "Yeah, Babe," I said, "mustard and mayo. The usual, the way we like 'em. Got somebody in the office. See ya soon. Bye."

Allyson had been glancing around the office while I talked to Margo, and I was able to compose myself somewhat. I don't know why I felt so guilty. There wasn't anything wrong with watching someone walk down the street, was there?

"So, Allyson," I said, "is there something I can do for you, or were you just checking out the rest of the building?"

"No, I did that a long time ago," she said. "Mother and I have been in this building for many years more than even your boss, as you probably know. We like what his ownership has meant to the place, and while I haven't been up here on the second floor for a couple of years, I'm not surprised to see that he runs a handsome office. But no, I'm here on business, I think."

"Well, he lives right here in the building, you know,"

I said. "Just down the hall. So he can kind of keep an eye on the agency that's supposed to be keeping an eye on it for him. I live here, too, just down from Earl."

Allyson nodded politely, and I wondered why I had said that. She couldn't have cared less. "I'm sorry," I said. "You're here on business?"

"I think."

"Right. How can I help you decide if you are or not?"

She smiled a huge smile that started slowly but was worth the wait. Her perfect teeth, full lips, and long, thin nose set off her wide-set green eyes and made her look as if she had been put together from a kit. She pressed her lips together to resume a serious demeanor. "Well, I have a problem, and I've debated for months whether I should seek help with it, pursue it myself, or just forget it. I've seen your sign downstairs but never worked up the nerve to come up here. This was hardly the day for it, being our biggest shopping day of the year, but I'm sort of impulsive and knew today was the day I would look you up."

I liked her already. She didn't appear the type who had to work up the courage to do anything, yet she admitted not only that but also that she was impulsive. I've never been the type who makes myself vulnerable with strangers, and the self-confidence that evidenced in her made her all the more attractive. I wanted to tell her that, but all that came out was, "The day after Thanksgiving is your biggest day of the year, huh?"

"Yeah. That's true with most places." She looked tolerant again.

"I'm sorry," I said. "I keep getting off your subject. Who'd you murder?"

Her bemused look returned, and I was suddenly apologizing again. "I know I shouldn't do that," I said. "Someday I'm going to say that to the wrong person and get an answer."

"I could get to like you, Mr.—?"

"Spence," I said. "Call me Philip."

"My problem is nothing like murder," she said, smiling. "And nothing like yours."

"I do have a problem, don't I?" I said.

"If that's your opening line with every prospective client, you do for sure."

We laughed.

"Are you really a prospective client?" I asked, trying to get serious.

"I think so."

"There you go again. Thinking. Let *us* do the thinking. Are you, or not?"

"There are a lot of things I'll want to know first," she said. "And there are a few things I'll want to tell you about me and my problem to see if you're interested. But your lunch is on its way, and I don't know if you're, I mean, are you the one who—"

"It's all right, Allyson. And no, I'm not the one who would screen you. Earl does that. I would probably sit in on it since you talked to me first, but Earl's the one you'll need to officially start with. You'll like him, and he'll be able to tell you if we can help you or not. I gotta admit I'm curious, but I won't ask. You can save it for him."

14

"I wouldn't mind telling you, Philip," she said, "but why don't you just tell Mr. Haymeyer that I would like you to sit in on our meeting."

"OK."

"And when will that be?"

I rummaged around Bonnie's desk, trying to find a note with Earl's schedule on it, and Allyson jumped up to open the door for Margo, who was balancing a cardboard tray of food.

"Thank you," Margo said, breezing in, delivering the food, and taking off her hat and coat seemingly in one move. "You're Allyson from the boutique, right?"

"Right," Allyson said, looking directly into Margo's eyes, the way she had mine. "And you must be Babe."

"Babe?" Margo and I repeated in unison.

"Isn't that what you called her on the phone?"

"Oh, yeah—no, this is Margo, an investigator on our staff. That's just what I call her. Babe."

"Don't let me interrupt," Margo said. "I have work I can do if you're talking, and there's nothing hot here that will suffer from getting cold."

"No, no," Allyson said. "I have to run, but I will be back to see Mr. Haymeyer—when, Philip?"

I turned back to my rummaging at Bonnie's desk, but Margo saved me the trouble. "Two-thirty," she said, "Give him half an hour and drop in at three. If we find he can't see you then, Bonnie will call you at the boutique."

"I appreciate it, Margo. And Philip." And she was gone.

15

I can't say I wasn't disappointed that Margo had shown up before Allyson and I had really finished talking. And that made me feel guilty.

"So you finally get to meet your dream girl," Margo teased.

"You're my dream girl, you know that," I said, leaning to kiss her. She offered only her cheek and grunted her disbelief.

"And was there some reason you didn't tell her why you call me 'Babe'?"

"I guess I assumed it was obvious. Sorry."

"Uh-huh. And how long was she here?"

"I don't know. Why?"

"Long enough that you should have asked to take her coat?"

I smacked an open palm on my forehead and turned toward the food. "Yeah." I shook my head.

"What's her problem?" Margo asked.

"Problem?"

"Well, she wasn't up here just to see you, was she?"

I laughed. "No, unfortunately." Margo was not amused. "I don't know. She's gonna tell Earl this afternoon. Where is he, anyway?"

"He and Larry are on a domestic case in Chicago, not far from Larry's apartment."

"I thought Earl didn't take domestic squabbles."

"It's more than a squabble, and it's a relative of Larry's. Bonnie knows more about it than I do. Ask her. You gonna pray before you're finished with that sandwich?"

" 'Spose I should."

"If you don't want God to give you a tummyache," she said.

I tossed a pickle at her.

"Anyway, you're gonna be finished with your lunch before I take a bite."

"Sorry." I reached for her hand, and we prayed.

I was tossing my garbage, and Margo was still munching when Bonnie returned. Late fifties, motherly, and superefficient, she was the office glue. But right now, she was crying.

Chapter Two

Margo hurried to Bonnie, helping with her coat and steadying her as she took off her boots. "What is it, Bon?" Margo said.

I turned my back to them and tried to look busy, but there was nowhere to escape except to the darkroom or Earl's office, and that would have looked phony.

"I lied to you, and I feel terrible," Bonnie blurted. "I'm not a lying person, you know that. It's not like me."

"Bonnie, sit down," Margo said. "Philip, will you catch the phone if it rings?" I sat at Bonnie's desk again, and Margo and Bonnie sat at mine.

"Now, what did you lie about? Whatever it was, I'm sure you had a good reason."

"I told you that domestic case Earl and Larry are working on concerned a relative of Larry's."

"Yes. And it doesn't?"

"No, it's my daughter!"

"Bonnie, it's all right. You don't have to be ashamed. We're with you. Do you want to talk about it?"

"I guess. It's hard living alone and seeing your

19

daughter's marriage failing and not having anyone to talk to about it."

"You know you can talk to us."

"Thanks, Margo. Well, it's Linda."

"Linda? The one we visited in Milwaukee last year?"

"Right."

"I would have thought—I mean—"

"I know—it's all right. I would have thought if one of my daughters was going to have trouble at home, it would be Tracy. She always was a pistol. But you know, she and Lew are happy as larks. 'Course, there are no little ones yet."

"Yeah. And Linda has the daughter, um—"

"Erin. She's thirteen now."

"Right. So, are things bad? Linda and Greg seemed so happy when we saw them."

"Well, you know Greg was never really thrilled with his job in Milwaukee, but Linda only reluctantly went along with the move back to Chicago. They were coming to a higher cost of living area for a sales job with lots of potential but less salary and commission to start."

"It was a risk."

"Yes, and one Greg was willing to take for the sake of his family. At least that's what I counseled Linda. No doubt I was being selfish. I had always dreamed of having Erin close enough to visit whenever I wanted. I don't even mind her staying with me when they're gone, but they aren't gone much—together anyway."

Bonnie turned away from Margo and stared out the

window. She pressed a tissue to her face and broke down again.

"Job pressures are always tough on a marriage, aren't they?" Margo tried.

"That's just it," Bonnie said. "It has nothing to do with the job itself. Linda was suspicious from the beginning about Greg's big sacrifice for the sake of her and Erin, and I guess she was right all along. I don't mind being wrong; I have no illusions about my judgment, but I kept telling Linda that Greg was doing it for her."

"And he wasn't?" Margo was trying to lead Bonnie without prying. I felt for her. It was a delicate spot. Bonnie obviously wanted to talk about it, but Margo didn't want to appear too eager.

"No, he sure wasn't," Bonnie said with a heavy sigh. "Maybe I should wait and see what Larry and Earl find before I start jumping to conclusions the way Linda has."

"What are Linda's conclusions?"

"Oh, she thinks Greg moved back to Chicago for an old girl friend."

"Oh, no."

"I'm afraid so. Her name is Carla. Greg was engaged to her when he was in college. Linda had met her once but had never worried about her until now."

"What makes her think Greg's seeing the girl now, after all these years?"

"She's only the boss's secretary in Greg's office."

"You're kidding. And Greg didn't know that when he took the job?"

"That's what he claims, but how could he not have known? He came to Chicago three different times about this job, and he was in the office every time. He had lunches and dinners with the sales staff and the big boss. You can't tell me he didn't know."

"But that's what he claims?"

"That's right. Linda says he hit her with it a few days after they had moved. He comes home from work and says, 'Guess who works in our office?' Some surprise, huh?

"Linda was steamed about it for a few days but kept telling me that even though she figured Greg knew Carla worked there, he had kept it from her just to protect her."

"But she's not giving him the benefit of the doubt anymore?"

"Hardly. Now she's convinced not only that Greg moved back to Chicago because Carla works here, but also that Carla recommended him and greased the wheels."

"Carla's not married?"

"She was once. No more—no kids—" She sighed. "A real number."

"Even if Greg did come because Carla was here, does that necessarily mean he has to be seeing her?"

"Not necessarily, but Linda is convinced he is. He's withdrawn, moody, irritable. He's gone a lot, blaming it on the work schedule. He's caught on that he should never mention Carla's name at home, so he doesn't. Not ever. That makes Linda even more suspicious. She tried to challenge him on it, accusing him of moving his family to Chicago for another woman, and he wouldn't deny it. He just blew up, told her she was crazy and if that's what she thought she ought to act on it."

"What did he mean by that?"

"That she should leave him, file for divorce, or something. I don't know. I've said enough."

"I can see why you're upset, Bonnie," Margo said. "Far be it from me to advise you, but I agree that you should be careful about judging Greg until you hear from Earl. You never really know what's going on."

"I know. And I will. It's just that I'm tired of trying to explain away his actions to Linda when she knows him so much better than I do. They've been married nearly fifteen years. They've had their problems, but this is a new one for me."

"How long has this been going on?"

"About six months."

"I'm amazed. You've known about it all this time?"

"Just about."

"You haven't let it affect your work."

Bonnie sat up straight, then rose. She dabbed her eyes and moved toward her desk. I smiled at her as I left her chair. "I would never let it affect my work, Margo," she said, sounding almost offended. "I take almost as much pride in my work as in anything else in my life."

"We know," Margo said, and I nodded. "And it shows."

Bonnie smiled gratefully and began to arrange her papers. I raised my eyebrows at Margo as I passed her on the way to my desk. I had just sat down when Earl arrived, reached for his messages, and nodded to everyone as he hustled back to his office. Usually there's a tendency for everyone in the office to line up at his door, waiting for an audience, but Margo and I figured Bonnie had the most pressing need for him. We were both a little surprised when she didn't follow him.

"I wish he wouldn't do that," she said. "Walk right past me with hardly any acknowledgment, especially when he knows I'm living and dying for some word."

Earl poked his head out.

"These two know what's going on?" he asked. He has a nose for knowing what people have been talking about. Of course, with Bonnie's red eyes, it didn't tax his investigative powers.

"Yeah," Bonnie said.

"Just as well," he said. "Hard to keep secrets around here. No need anyway, I guess."

"Right," Bonnie said.

"Well, there's not much to tell, Bon. Larry's gonna stay on it tonight as late as he has to. He and I saw very little today. Greg went out to lunch with the boss and Carla and a couple of other people. There were five of them, two women. Nothing inappropriate that we could see. I'll say this, though, if I were Greg's wife, I wouldn't want him going out to lunch with Carla in a group of a hundred."

That didn't comfort Bonnie much, but still she

thanked Earl. He and Larry were donating valuable agency time to a domestic problem, the very type of a case Earl never accepts. "Can't pay me enough to follow unfaithful spouses around to bars and hotels," he had said more than once. But as a freebie, and for the best secretary and receptionist he'd ever had: anything.

"Whose lousy handwriting is this, Philip?" Earl called from his office a few minutes later.

Bonnie and Margo enjoyed that, and I grimaced. Earl appeared in his doorway again with my Allyson Scheel note in his hand. "You just got licensed to carry a handgun, didn't you, Philip?"

"Yeah."

"We're gonna have to go out and get you a piece this afternoon, but if you shoot the way you scribble, I'm in as much trouble as you are. Now, who is this, and why does he or she want to see me at three P.M.?"

"Allyson Scheel. She's the—"

"The good-looker from the boutique, yeah?" Earl said, suddenly studying the note carefully. "What does she want?"

"I don't know. I didn't talk to her long. She just dropped in and said she had a problem and was thinking about talking to us about it."

"C'mon, Philip, you usually do better than that. I appreciate your letting her know that I handle the initial interviews—you did tell her that, didn't you?—but you usually give me a little to go on, something to look for, something to expect."

Margo cut in. "Excuse me, chief, but I think it's safe

to say that your junior colleague was just a little intimidated by Miss Scheel and didn't handle the conversation in his usual professional style."

"Is that right, Philip?" Earl said with a grin. "I can't say I blame you." As he turned back to his desk he called over his shoulder, "Bonnie, please call Miss Scheel at the Beatrice Boutique downstairs and tell her I can't see her until four this afternoon. Philip, give me a few minutes, and then let's go shopping."

It was always sort of fun to watch, or at least hear, Earl at work. He could get more done in fifteen minutes with a dictating machine and the telephone than most people could accomplish in half a day. He sped through correspondence and details so he would have time to think, to ponder, to pore over files and notes on cases. "Thinking is the life's blood of our profession," he would remind us. "Don't get bogged down in clerical work."

Earl was a mover, always on the run. I listened closely for the end of his last phone call because when I heard the familiar squeak of the chair celebrating his leaving it, I reached for my coat. If I didn't he would wing past me and would be out the door, down the stairs, and in the car by the time I got started. And here he came.

I fell in behind him, pulling my coat on. I blew a kiss to Margo and waved to Bonnie. Earl backed out of his parking space as I was shutting the passenger side door. "So, how do you feel about this, kid?" he wanted to know.

"About getting a gun? I don't like it. You know that."

"You've always said that, Philip, and you've been with me nearly two years without any pressure to get one, but now that you've had your training and your orientation to shooting and everything, there's nothing standing in your way. Is there?"

"I've never needed a weapon. You've always told me this isn't like on TV where the guys are shooting out someone's tires between commercials."

"You're right, and you know I haven't fired my gun in the line of duty in twenty years."

"I know your rule of never drawing your gun unless you're prepared to shoot, and never shooting unless you're shooting to kill."

"It's a good basic rule, Philip, and I live by it. Whenever you can avoid shooting someone, whenever you can subdue him by any other means, that's what you want to do."

"So why am I buying a gun?"

"You're not. I'm buying it. But you're going to carry it, and it's going to be valuable to you, even if you never use it."

"It still makes me uncomfortable."

"It did me too, at first. Now I wouldn't feel comfortable in church without one."

"You don't go to church anyway."

"You know what I mean."

Earl parked in front of a sporting goods store, but suddenly wasn't in such a hurry. "Tell me," he said, "how are things between you and Margo?"

"OK, I guess."

27

"Really?"

"Yeah."

"Only OK?"

"Yeah."

"But OK?"

"Yes!"

"Then why hasn't she been wearing her engagement ring for the last three days?"

Chapter Three

I was speechless.

"Are you tellin' me *you* haven't noticed?"

I shook my head.

"I don't mind telling you, Philip, I care about you two."

"I know," I managed.

"But you can't, you must not, let your love problems interfere with your work."

"They won't, Earl. You can depend on that, but I don't know what this is all about. I hope I'll find out she's got dishpan hands or isn't used to wearing it in cold weather or something. It's not like her to stop wearing it and just hope I'll notice."

"No, it doesn't sound like her. That's why I figured you knew."

"I hate to admit I hadn't noticed. I guess I just took it for granted."

"Well, hey, if you're not aware of any problems, it's probably nothing. Sorry I brought it up." Earl started to get out of the car but hesitated when he noticed I wasn't moving.

"I'm not saying I'm not aware that she's had second thoughts," I said. "We've done a lot of serious talking lately. She's not interested in anyone else, and she says it isn't that she doesn't still love me or anything like that. But she did want a cooling-off period."

"Well, that's it then," Earl said, uncomfortable in a counselor's role, especially on this topic.

"No, that's not it, Earl," I said. "I thought we had agreed not to have a cooling-off period yet. We've both been working on important cases, and we didn't want any emotional strain right now. I agreed to quit pressuring her for a wedding date, and she agreed to hold off on any moratorium on the relationship."

"Well, you'd better find out what's going on then, Philip. I don't need to know. I just want what's best for both of you, and I don't want to lose either of you, regardless what happens. Have you thought about how awkward it might be to work in the same office if your relationship changed?"

"Earl, Margo and I go back a long, long way, maybe not in terms of years, but we've been through a ton of trauma."

"I know that. Maybe that's why she needs a break. But have you thought about what I said?"

"No. It never crossed my mind. Sure I've thought about what it would be like in the office if we were in limbo for a while, but I never even considered the possibility that she would sever the relationship."

"And *you* would never sever it?"

"Of course not."

"Don't you think she opens the possibility of its ending when she proposes a moratorium?"

"I hope not."

"You're being naive. And I'm out of my field. Just know that I'm concerned, more for the two of you than just keeping our super team together, but that *is* important."

"I know. And thanks, Earl."

"Sure. Let's buy a gun."

It was hard to concentrate on the sales pitch from the clerk, but I was brought back to the present when he whispered that he could "work it out" if we didn't have licenses.

"We have licenses," Earl said, "because we are private investigators who care about the law, particularly handgun laws."

"Oh, certainly, yessir. I do too. I just meant that—"

"I know what you meant, partner," Earl said. "And if you want a quick sale, forget the rest of the pieces and show us a Colt snubnosed .38."

The clerk became quietly efficient then and pulled a handsome box out from under the counter. Even a passive type like me had to admit that it was a beautiful handgun, as handguns go. It was heavy in my hand as I had remembered from the practice range. "It's a powerful mass of metal, Philip," Earl said. "I've always been able to sense its potential violence just by holding it."

"I know what you mean," I said. It was cold, blue-black, threatening. "What do you want to hear, Earl? If this is what you want me to carry, I'll carry it."

"Do you want a belt, pocket, or shoulder holster?" the clerk asked. I looked to Earl.

"Carrying it on your belt or in your pocket, especially the way you feel about it, will make you constantly aware of it. It can get in the way when you sit and stand and get in and out of the car. With a shoulder holster, once you get the hang of slipping it on and off each day and get used to the feel of the straps, you'll wear the gun without thinking about it. It'll fit between your ribs and your stomach and will be out of sight."

"That's what I want," I said.

Earl pulled out his credit card and the papers showing that I was licensed to carry a concealed weapon, that it would be registered in the name of the EH Detective Agency, but that I would be the sole user. I was amazed that the total price, including ammunition, was more than two hundred dollars.

"It's the confidence," Earl said, carefully loading the pistol. "It evens the score. You have a last ditch form of extremely efficient protection should you ever need it. It makes alleys less dark, strange places less strange. It slows your pulse a few thumps during tense situations. You'll get used to having it, Philip."

"I hope so."

It was nearly three-thirty by the time we returned to the office. Bonnie told Earl that Miss Scheel would see him at four. "I forgot to tell you she wanted me in on that, Earl," I said, "if it's OK."

"Sure."

I found it difficult to look at Margo. She looked up from her work and smiled a greeting as I approached, but I didn't hide my emotions well. I leaned over her desk. "Would you tell me why you're not wearing your ring?" I whispered urgently.

"Yes, but not here, not now, Philip. Later, OK?"

"I don't know if it's OK or not," I said. "I know what we've been discussing, but no one here knows, I hope." I knew that sounded like an accusation, but I couldn't help it. She shook her head to assure me that she had discussed our business with no one.

"But they sure know when you don't wear your ring for a few days," I said.

"Did *you* notice?"

"No, frankly, I didn't. Earl asked me about it. Can you imagine how it made me feel? Margo, you have the right to do anything you want and make any decisions you want, but don't you feel you owe it to me to tip me off when you decide to quit wearing your ring? It looks like we've broken our engagement. Is that what you want?"

"I don't know."

"Well, it's obviously what you want it to look like."

"I'm *sorry*, Philip," she said, sounding more defensive than sorry. "I didn't intend it to look like anything. I've been going through some real doubts about myself and us, and I just didn't feel like wearing the ring the last few days. I was relieved when you didn't notice. I didn't want to hurt you, and I thought if the feeling passed or I came up with some answers, I would start wearing it

33

again. Do you understand?"

"No, I don't. Not everyone in this office is as unobservant a detective as I am. Earl probably noticed the first day. He said this is the third day you haven't worn it."

"He's right," she said.

"I'm hurt."

"I'm *sorry*."

"I wonder."

"Now *I'm* hurt, Philip. Whatever other problems we have, I don't need you accusing me of lying."

"You're right," I said, stealing a glance to see if Bonnie could hear us. "It's just that you don't sound sorry, and not wearing your diamond without even discussing it with me is insensitive."

"We discussed my doubts, Philip."

"But you never mentioned not wearing the ring."

"I suggested a cooling-off period."

"But I thought we had decided to put that off!"

"A cooling-off period on the cooling-off period? Yes, I guess we did, but I just can't put my feelings in the deep freeze until our work schedule gets lighter. Who knows when that'll be? Philip, I think we need to take the time to discuss this and get it settled."

"A moratorium on our engagement doesn't sound like a settlement to me."

"That's because you don't want it."

"And you do?"

"Of course I do."

"Then you're right we'd better talk about it," I said.

"How about tonight at dinner? Earl is concerned that we don't let our problems get in the way of our work."

"So you don't want me to say anything to anyone here about our problems, yet you discuss them with Earl?"

"He brought it up, Margo! He noticed you weren't wearing your ring."

"And he's more concerned with the work than with us?"

"You know better than that."

"Do I? You know, Philip, talking about splitting with you, even temporarily, is a scary thing. I'm nearly an orphan without you. If I have to worry that Earl is going to throw me—or us—out unless we get married—"

"I'll set you straight about how Earl feels about it tonight, OK? Where do you want to go?"

"Anywhere quiet. Don't spend a lot of money, especially when I'm feeling this way. You deserve better than that."

"I'm worried about you, Margo."

"So am I."

"Mostly I'm curious about why you were so offended that I didn't tell Allyson we were engaged when it's apparent you wish we weren't anyway."

"I don't know, Philip. I don't even understand myself. That's one of the reasons I want a break, not an end. It would be unfair to both of us for me to dump you when I'm not sure of my own feelings. That's the point."

"I'll pick you up at seven tonight," I said.

I made some final notes on a case I had finished investigating the day before and delivered the documents to Bonnie to be typed for Earl. Then I told him I thought I was free for another assignment, and we were chatting in his office when Bonnie buzzed him and announced Allyson Scheel.

"Maybe this will be your next case, Philip," he said. "Are you going to be up to it, regardless what happens with Margo over the next few days?"

"Sure," I said. But I wasn't sure.

Allyson looked exquisite as ever. I adjusted my chair so I could watch her when she talked. I had to remind myself not to keep staring when Earl was talking. She had to be used to people's watching her, though. I wondered if she had ever been through an ugly duckling stage. Someday I would ask her.

"You've met Mr. Spence," Earl said as he directed her to a chair.

"Philip," I reminded her.

"And I'm Earl Haymeyer. You can call me Earl, or Mr. Haymeyer, whatever you're most comfortable with. Anyway, what can we do for you? We're eager to help in whatever way we can, short of investigating domestic quarrels."

"Well, no, it's nothing like that," Allyson said, crossing her legs and interlocking her fingers. "Do you mind if I ask some questions about you and your agency first?"

"Not at all. Please."

"Since it's a small firm, could you tell me about the backgrounds of your people?"

"It's pretty simple," Earl began. "I've been in

detective work for about twenty years, first as a local police officer, then as a special investigator for the US attorney's office. I started this agency a couple of years ago with Philip, who was a commercial free-lance artist before that and whom I trained from scratch. He has also had a professional training course since joining us, as has Margo Franklin, who also started without experience. She is studying criminology in night school.

"Larry Shipman was a free-lance communications expert in radio, television, and print journalism, and had worked often with our office as an undercover agent when I was with the US attorney. Despite the limited backgrounds of these three, each has distinguished himself over the past two years, and I'm proud of how each has progressed. I would trust any one of them with just about any case."

"Even mine?"

"I haven't even heard it yet, but yes, even yours."

Chapter Four

"I start every investigation with the proper paper-work," Earl explained, pulling from his desk drawer a manila folder and a pad of forms entitled EH Detective Agency Client Registration. From another drawer he produced a black felt marker and printed A. SCHEEL in neat block letters on the folder.

"I'm going to ask you a few questions," he said. "You may refuse to answer any that you wish, but I want to make clear that every answer is helpful to us and that we pledge one hundred percent confidentiality. I also want you to know that if in the course of our investigation we find that anything you tell us here has been intentionally misleading, we drop the case."

Allyson nodded but appeared uneasy. "I have no reason to lie to you, Mr. Haymeyer," she said.

"I'm sure you don't. I just want you to know how important this preliminary questioning is. We base much of our work on the mundane facts we get from the client, and if those facts are wrong, it will cost us time and you money. And if they were intentionally wrong, we simply don't have time to mess with it. It's difficult enough to investigate a problem without having to investigate the client as well."

"I understand," Allyson said.

Earl placed his pad of forms over the manila folder and pulled a black, ball-point pen from his shirt pocket. "Full name please," he said.

Allyson glanced my way with a slight smile, almost as if she was beginning to enjoy this. I knew the feeling. "Allyson Abigail Scheel," she said.

"Date and place of birth?"

"August 31, 1954, Chicago."

"Home address?"

"Old Depot Towers, One Green Bay Court, Wilmette, Illinois."

"Occupation?"

"Co-owner, with my mother, of the Beatrice Boutique, Glencoe Road, Glencoe."

"Nature of the business and your role?"

"We sell designer fashions, mostly imported. I'm the buyer."

"Annual income?"

Allyson flinched.

"Let me tell you why I ask," Earl said. "There are people who can't afford us, and we either help them find assistance, or we are able to charge reduced rates in special instances."

"I understand. That won't be necessary. I assumed when I came up here that this would be expensive."

"Not terribly," Earl said. "We charge two hundred ninety per day for up to twenty-four hours when necessary."

"Do you still need to know my income?" Allyson said.

Earl nodded. "It would be helpful."

"It depends on the year," Allyson said. "For the last two years Mother and I have drawn sixty-five thousand dollars each from the business. This year we're planning to draw closer to seventy-five thousand each. I do appreciate your pledge of confidence about that." I was still shaking my head.

"The nature of your problem?" Earl continued.

"It's hard to explain, Mr. Haymeyer," Allyson said, settling more comfortably in her chair. "I suppose it won't be the type of investigation you're used to. There's no crime, no villain. At least I hope there's not. It's just that for as wonderful as my life is and has been, there are gaps in my history—centering on my father—and I want to put the pieces together."

"I'm not sure I follow," Earl said. "Is your father living?"

"Oh, yes."

"Are your parents still married?"

"No, they divorced when I was a baby."

"I want you to tell me this story, Allyson. Tell me anything you want and don't make me fish for information. If I need to know something, I'll ask. Otherwise, I want you to tell me just what your problem is and exactly how you feel we can help you."

"OK."

"Do you mind if I tape this, for our purposes only?"

"I guess not."

41

Earl leaned back in his chair and opened a cabinet behind him, revealing a huge reel-to-reel tape recorder. He flipped it on and shut the cabinet. "The microphone will pick you up. Just go ahead," he said.

"Well, my first memories of my father were of meeting him at the train station in Wilmette. He was, and still is, a garment cutter in Chicago, and he still lives in the four-room flat on the West Side where he and my mother lived after they were married in 1952. Following their divorce in 1955, Mother and I moved to a small apartment in Wilmette and she worked as a dress design trainee in a small store in Kenilworth.

"She didn't talk much about my father, and I didn't ask much at first. All I know is that from as far back as I can remember, she and I would walk ten blocks to the train station the last Sunday of every other month and would meet Curtis Scheel as he stepped off the train. He always dressed the same. He still does. He wears black oxford shoes with thick rubber soles that must last eight or ten years. His suits are drab and dark, and he probably has never owned more than three at one time. They are hard to tell apart. The pants have cuffs, the coats are singlebreasted and always buttoned, and he always wears sweater vests over white shirts and a plain dark tie.

"As a child I thought him strange. He spoke with a thick accent that I learned was German. He always wore a hat, even in the summer, and he always carried himself formally, but not necessarily with dignity. There were no airs about him. In fact, he would not be noticed in any crowd. He was always neat and clean and closely shaved, and his hands were always immaculate. They still are. I tell you, Mr. Haymeyer, it's hard to separate what he was then from what he is now, because other than the loss of some of his hair and the graying of what's left, he appears the same."

Earl interrupted. "Do you mind if I stand as I listen?" he said. "I won't if it bothers you."

"Not at all," she said. "Am I getting anywhere?"

"I don't know. I'm not sure yet. But please continue."

"Well, anyway, I began to look forward to those visits. When I was tiny, two months between visits seemed so long that I couldn't put it into perspective. After he visited, I would badger my mother for days to tell me when he was coming again, but I didn't understand answers like 'in fifty days,' and things like that. By the time he returned, I would have almost given up hope of seeing him again."

"But you wanted to see him? These visits were enjoyable for you?"

"Oh, yes! I had not yet put together the idea that other kids had live-in fathers and I didn't. I'm not sure I even knew that a father was the male equivalent of a mother. A mother was the only person you knew from forever, and a father was a small, shy, formal man who hugged you tight and cried when he met you at the train station every other month.

"He would kiss me all over my face and hold me like he never wanted to let go, and then we would walk back to our apartment where my mother fixed dinner and I played on the floor with my father until it was time for my nap. When I woke up, we had a light meal, and then Mother and I walked him back to the train. There he would hug me and kiss me and cry again. Once I said, 'Bye-bye, Daddy,' and he firmly but kindly told me, 'I'm not your daddy. I'm your father. Call me Father.' I said, 'OK, Father. Come and see me again soon.'"

Earl had been standing with his arms crossed, staring intently down at Allyson. Now he walked slowly over to the window and thrust his hands deep into his pockets. He appeared depressed, but Allyson wouldn't have been able to tell. She stopped speaking when he moved to the window, but he gestured that she should continue. She turned in her chair to face him, but it must have been disconcerting to address his back. He was staring at the sunset, yet hardly seemed to notice it. I found Allyson's story a little sad too, but I wasn't hearing it through Earl's ears. He was a widower whose only son was autistic. Even a strained, on-again off-again relationship between parent and child was more than he had enjoyed with a son who had never recognized him.

"As I got older," Allyson said, "I was able to understand what my father and mother talked about during those every-other-month Sunday dinners. He asked once in a while to take me back to his place, but she refused. Their divorce had been amicable. They were not at all hostile to each other. She was cordial to him, but she made it clear that she would not let me visit him at his apartment until I was older, and that she didn't care to go there with me. 'Let's just keep it going this way,' she suggested. He was not a fighter. He never argued with her. Sometimes he would just beg to have me to himself. I wished for that, too, but my mother was protective and didn't want things to change.

"Which they didn't until I was in sixth grade. Every time my father had visited for the previous year or so, I had peppered him with questions about his past. I was developing a curiosity about this man, and I never got the answers I wanted and needed. My mother finally told me that the marriage had simply not worked out. Neither had been mean to the other. There had been no fights. It just didn't work out. I couldn't understand that. If you got along, you could stay married—that was my idea.

"And my schoolmates mostly had two parents at home. I was embarrassed that my parents were divorced, but I bragged about my father and made up stories about him to make him appear even more romantic to my friends. I told them that he brought me expensive gifts every month, when in truth he brought me trinkets. At Christmas I would get something nice, but I couldn't understand why my father was never at our family gatherings. My mother's family is Irish-American and have loud, happy celebrations. They don't like my father and don't invite him, but she told me—and he later confirmed this—that he doesn't care to come anyway. That was when I asked him why I had so many aunts and uncles and cousins and even two grandparents on my mother's side, and none on his side."

"They were all in Germany still?" Earl said, his back still to Allyson.

"No," she said. "He said he was an orphan and never knew his parents. He had virtually no relatives. It was so sad I could hardly take it in. Then I wanted to know everything about the orphanage where he grew up, but he said it was too painful and that he had shut out all the memories. I wanted to know how he had come to the United States, and he said he had just saved his money until he could get a ticket to sail here. He said he found New York too big and Chicago not much better, but he had no more money to keep moving, so he settled and found a job with the trade he had been taught in technical high school.

"I'll never forget the night when I was in junior high and I asked my mother to tell me everything she knew about my father. I couldn't stand those sketchy ending-the-discussion stories I had heard all my life. I loved my father, but I resented that he had no roots. I felt life had been unfair to him and thus to me. He had no family, and so I had no family on his side."

"And so did your mother tell you anything you hadn't picked up before?" Earl said, finally turning to face Allyson.

"Did she ever."

Chapter Five

It was dark outside. Bonnie knocked softly and opened Earl's door. "I'm heading home unless there's anything else, boss," she said, smiling and winking at Allyson.

"Thanks, Bonnie," Earl said. "I think we're all right. See you tomorrow."

"Margo's going home with me, Philip," Bonnie said. "She told me to tell you that if she didn't hear from you by five-thirty she'd take a rain check and not to worry about it."

"OK," I said quickly, hoping that Allyson wouldn't assume that Margo and I were going together. That made me feel despicable, but I was feeling sorry for myself because of Margo's attitude, and I found myself hoping I could keep my options open. I nearly shook my head, disgusted with myself.

Bonnie pulled the door shut behind her, and Earl asked if either of us was hungry. "I'm good until about eight o'clock," Allyson said.

"Me too," I said, wanting to have something in common with her.

"Feel up to continuing?" Earl said.

"Sure. Mother told me she had met my father while she was touring a garment factory as part of a class she was taking. The students weren't supposed to talk to the cutters and the others on the line, but she said Father looked so sad and shy and withdrawn that he was a challenge. She had been the spark plug of the class, the witty, funny, loud one, so when she had a question for the tour guide, she asked it and then insisted that Father answer it. He blushed and demurred, but before the tour guide could rescue him, Mother went right over to his table and said, 'C'mon now, we both know you're gonna be running this place someday. Tell me what happens when you feel a cloth shipment price is too high. Do you bargain, do you go elsewhere, or do you just refuse to buy until the price comes down?'

"The class was tittering and clapping, enjoying the show, and Father brought the house down when he said, just above a whisper, 'I don't have not'ing to do wit' cutting da prices. I cut only da cloth.' There was an uproar as Mother threw her arms around him and kissed him on the cheek. 'You're a good sport, man,' she said, and as she walked back to the group she said, loudly enough that he could hear, 'I wouldn't mind seeing him again sometime.' When the laughter died down, Father was heard to say, 'You know vere to reach me. Dis is vere I am everyday.'

"Mother told me that, to the astonishment of her friends, she went back to the factory two days later and waited for Father at the gate. He almost turned white before he turned crimson, but she was so drawn to him that she just took over, insisting upon showing him the town. She got more money from her father, who was putting her through school, than he earned as a garment cutter, so she even financed their first night out on the town. They went up to the top of the Prudential Building, they visited the lakefront, they walked up and down State Street, and they went to the movies.

"Mother says he was very quiet even that night, but it was obvious that he loved the attention. I don't know if you've seen my mother—" we both nodded "—then you know she's a very attractive woman. Here was a small, shy, immigrant laborer being dragged around the city by a beautiful Irish-American. She could have had any guy she wanted, and was asked out all the time, but she began to turn down everyone else. If she didn't hear from Curt often enough, she'd call him. He never became very conversant, but she had won his heart, and he had won hers. Her family couldn't believe the match and refused to consent to the marriage. They predicted divorce, which had not tainted the family name for generations, but my parents were married anyway, alone, before a justice of the peace."

"Is that why your mother never remarried?" Earl asked. "Family pressure?"

"Partly, I suppose. But she is a woman of such high moral standards, I think she feels she doesn't have the right to remarry as long as my father is alive. I know that sounds old-fashioned, but I think that's how she feels. Her family is Catholic, and she has never even dated, to my knowledge, since the divorce more than twenty-five years ago."

"Can I ask a question, Earl?" I said.

"Sure."

"What caused the divorce—the lack of things in common, the different cultural backgrounds, the big difference in personalities, what?"

"This is the strange part, Philip," Allyson said. "My mother finally told me that the reason she divorced my father was that she was as frustrated by being shut out of his former life as I was. She told me she couldn't penetrate that memory, she couldn't get past the obscure orphanage in Berlin, a city big enough to have dozens of orphanages. She heard no names of friends, relatives, or even acquaintances."

"But that's not enough to cause a divorce," Earl said. "Frustrating, yes. Something that would lead a spirited woman to despair, sure. But divorce?"

"There was more than that, Mr. Haymeyer," Allyson said. "It was not simply that my father had no family and no history. It was that he maintained this posture despite recurring nightmares that scared my mother to death. He would scream out in the darkness, clutching his pillow, pleading for his life, calling out in German she could hardly understand. He would not even wake himself up. He might rise and calm down, and go to the other room and sit for long periods, but he never admitted to remembering the bad dreams the next day.

"My mother says she badgered him, 'You mean to tell me you don't know that you woke the neighbors with your screams in the night?'

"And he would say, 'Nonsense.'

"She would ask him what certain German words meant, and he would cloud over and become sullen. She had a way of getting the definitions out of him, but she always regretted it. What he was saying in terror were things like, 'Wait! Don't! Please! Mama! Father! I'm sorry! Your blood is on my hands!'

"She begged him to tell her what it all meant. The closest he ever came to convincing her was when he said that if her accounts were true of his terror in the night, perhaps it was something common to orphans who never knew their parents.

"She didn't want to hurt him or falsely accuse him, but she suggested to him once the possibility that he had harmed his parents or even killed them and had been sent to an orphanage after that. He refused to discuss it, except to say that he had been told all his life that his parents had died when he was an infant. By murder, accident, illness, he didn't know.

"My mother finally got to the point, when she was pregnant with me and had been married for two-and-a-half years, that she couldn't take it anymore. There was too much hidden in the man, too many dark secrets, too much pain and sorrow and despair. She was depressed. She loved him, yet she couldn't bring him out. Then she wondered if she really wanted to. She was afraid of what she might find beneath the surface of his personality. She begged him to see a psychiatrist, but he would have nothing to do with it. Sometimes he would sit for an hour, staring into space and crying softly, hardly aware he was doing it. Occasionally my mother would joke

51

with him, tousle his hair, treat him the way she had when they were courting. Then he would smile faintly and tell her that he loved her and couldn't live without her and would do anything for her. He told her she was the only flower in his life, yet he refused to seek help or to even tell her what was wrong.

" 'Do you deny that you are a man with deep pain?' she would demand.

" 'I cannot deny that,' he would say.

" 'Do you not want to be healed of this hurt?'

" 'Nothing can heal the pain of the soul,' he would say, 'especially when I don't know where the pain comes from. Perhaps it is common to orphans.'

"She had heard enough. She told him she wanted to hear no more of his past unless he told her the truth. She accused him of having his name changed when he came to the United States. No one in Germany spells Kurt with a 'C,' she would remind him. He said it was common for immigrants to Americanize their names.

"Finally my mother told him that she could not go on. She extended an unending offer to come back to him, to help him, to do anything he wanted her to do, and even to love him again if he would but be truthful with himself and seek help. She began sleeping in the other room, and after I was born, she never slept with him again. When one of his nightmares woke me one night, she asked him one last time to let her help him. When he refused, we moved out. Six months later her divorce was granted. She and my father worked out the visitation program, no alimony was involved, and that was that.

"I was raised by my mother, my father visited when she allowed, and he begged to have me visit him rather than his always visiting us. When I was a freshman in high school, she finally relented. He had visited like clockwork for years, and now she was going to let me take the train to the Chicago and North Western Station downtown, where he would meet me. It was no small sacrifice on her part. She worried herself sick over me. It was the fall of 1968, and there had been race riots in Chicago. She would not let me stay overnight at his place, and I didn't want to, anyway, fearing I would hear him cry out in the night."

"What kinds of visits were those?" Earl asked. "What did he have in common with you, and what did you talk about?"

"They were formal and uncomfortable. I loved him, and I knew he loved me deeply, but since my mother had told me the stories, I was wary of him, almost afraid of him. He would ask me about school and my plans for the future. By then my mother was assistant manager of a store and was making decent money. She talked of buying her own store someday and training me to be her partner and buyer. There was nothing I wanted more. 'That's good, that's good,' Father would say, every time I told him about the plans.

"That's when I told him that Mother thought it would be good if I spent my last two years of high school overseas to learn fashion design and the whole business. My father fell silent and then gravely asked me if he could tell me a secret. I began to tremble. Was he going

53

to tell me something he had not even told my mother when she had been his wife for nearly three years?

" 'Yes,' I whispered, frightened. 'I will keep your secret.' And I have kept it, Mr. Haymeyer. I have not even told my mother, who probably deserves to hear it. I have told no one in the world. Until now."

Chapter Six

Earl had been leaning against his bookcase for a long time, and he moved back to his desk and sat on its edge, dangling one leg over the side. He was a couple of feet from Allyson, whose face was taut. Her body appeared relaxed, except for her fingers, which were interlocked again, knuckles white. I felt an urge to put my arm around her, to comfort her, to encourage her to keep talking. She seemed so vulnerable.

I knew what was going through Earl's mind, because I'd heard him say it before after hearing someone's story: "It was impressive, but I don't see how we can help." I hoped he wouldn't say that this time, because I wanted to help. I didn't even know what Allyson wanted, but whatever it was, I wanted to be in on it.

"My father pointed into his bedroom, and I stood in the doorway as he shuffled in and knelt by his bed, pulling a shoebox from beneath it. He brought it out and we sat on his heavy old couch. He opened the box and then quickly closed it again, rose, and went back to his bedroom. He returned with another shoebox, opened it, and showed me various amounts of cash in small bills, a brochure from a travel agency, and a savings account book.

" 'I'm going to take a leave of absence one of these days and return to my homeland for several weeks,' he announced, his accent still thick after all those years in the States. He had less than a hundred and fifty dollars in his savings account, and the cash still left him short of two hundred dollars. 'It will take me another few years,' he said, more excited than I had seen him in ages, 'but I will get there.'

" 'What will you do there, Father?' I asked him. 'If you have no family, what is there for you?'

" 'You don't understand,' he said. 'We are talking about my homeland. My homeland. When you have no family and no wife, your homeland is your family.' He began to cry, and I embraced him, which had the opposite effect than I intended. He held me close and cried out in great wrenching sobs, 'Allyson Abigail, you are the only flesh and blood I have left who loves me. There is no one else! Don't leave this country for schooling overseas unless you go when I go.' "

" 'But, Father,' I said, 'Mother is sending me in just a couple of years. Will you be ready to go by then?'

"He shook his head sadly, turned away from me, and said, 'No.' I spent my two years overseas, and he never really forgave me for it. Oh, he was thrilled when I returned, but there was a sad distance between us that had never existed before."

"And did he ever get back to Germany?" Earl asked.

"No, but he hasn't given up. That's the reason I'm here. He told me recently that after all the years he's served his company, he has been able to combine three weeks of vacation and a brief leave of absence with no fear of losing seniority, and he will be leaving in two weeks for his homeland."

Allyson acted as if she had finished her story, catching Earl and me by surprise. "Why did he want this kept from your mother?" Earl said.

"I'm not sure. I think he feared that she would see hope in his visit, perhaps want to go with him and trace his family history, see the orphanage, or whatever."

"Why does he fear that?"

"I don't know. I honestly believe that after all these years, my mother still loves him and would be happy to be his wife again if he would get these haunting threads from his past tied together."

"Are you serious?" Earl asked, incredulous. "That's a long time."

"Absolutely," Allyson said. "She's never said anything like that, and she's never acted affectionately toward him in my presence, but by the same token, she has never once run him down. I think she merely pities him and remains frustrated by his refusal to seek help. She feels she did all she could before she gave up. There's certainly no one else in her life."

Earl pushed in his desk chair and offered Allyson her coat. "Let's all go get something to eat, and then you tell us how we can help. If one of us trails your father overseas, our daily price is increased by fifty percent. I'm sorry to talk business after that story of yours, but I wanted you to be aware of it."

On the way down to Earl's car, he continued, "One

57

thing I'm puzzled about is why you need someone other than yourself to follow him. He'd probably be thrilled to have you go along."

"That's just it," Allyson said. "There's more to the story. He's not going to Germany."

"Where *is* he going?" I said.

I opened the front passenger door for Allyson and then got in the back on the same side. I slid all the way over behind Earl so I had a better angle from which to talk to—OK, to see—Allyson, and I noticed Earl's amused look in the rearview mirror. He knew exactly what I was up to.

"I'm not sure where Father is going," Allyson said. "But it's not Germany. He's not booked on any flights out of O'Hare to Germany. He's booked on one to Kennedy Airport in New York, but nothing to Germany from there."

"So, you're a little detective yourself, huh?" I said with admiration.

"Oh, it didn't take much to track that down. I just want to know where he's going."

"Really?" I said. "Is that all? You don't want us to follow him?"

"Depends on where he's going," she said.

Earl pulled into the restaurant parking lot and turned off the engine. He turned sideways in his seat and faced Allyson. "Something's still sticking in my craw," he said. "A person who is inquisitive by nature, like you are, and a person who cares so much about her father and his history, like you do, is not going to let that first shoebox go. Didn't you wonder about it? Didn't you

58

think maybe there was something in there he didn't want you to see? I don't get it, Allyson. Why didn't you go after that box one day when the situation was right?"

"I did," she said, opening her door. "Aren't I a good girl? I'll tell you all about it."

Earl and I waited in the lobby for a table while Allyson excused herself for a few minutes. "What do you think?" I said.

"I dunno," he said, as if he wished he really did know. "She's got a real mystery here, and I need to take the time to think it through, listen to the tape again, see what it's all about."

"But are you interested in following her father to Germany or wherever just to find out why she doesn't have any relatives?"

"No, there's got to be more to it than that. I mean the undying curiosity of the orphan or the daughter of the orphan is just not enough to spur Allyson into investing in our services. She could find out that stuff herself, and I'm a little surprised she hasn't been to Germany already to do just that. I'm guessing that she or her mother, or both, already have a hypothesis she wants to try out on us. If she thinks her father is someone or has done something bad and she wants us to check that out, then, yes, I'd be interested in following him wherever he goes. In the US, that is."

"What do you mean, 'in the US?' Are you saying you wouldn't fulfill the wishes of a client willing to pay for international work?"

"Of course not. I'm just saying that *I* would follow

him in the States. If he leaves this country, he's yours."

"You're kidding."

"Would I kid you?"

"Yeah."

"But not this time. You want a good case, a little travel, an important assignment? This could be it, but don't start banking on it. If all she has is what she's told us already, I'll be declining the case. I can't afford to be chasing ambiguous puzzles where the clients give you nothing to go on and you're not even sure what they want you to find."

The hostess approached. "A table for three is ready for you, Mr. Haymeyer."

Earl looked quickly for Allyson. "I'll watch for her," I said. "I need to call Margo at Bonnie's anyway. We'll find you."

Bonnie answered just as Allyson came out of the women's washroom. I pointed her toward Earl. She winked her thanks, my heart skipped, and I said, "Hello, Allyson?"

"Uh, no, Philip," Bonnie said. "Who did you call?"

"Sorry. I just wanted to tell you, I mean Margo, that I was sorry I couldn't make dinner and that I appreciated her willingness to take a rain check."

"You can tell her. Just a minute."

I repeated the message to Margo. She was cool, but not unkind. "I know you want some straight answers from me, Philip. And I think I'm ready to give them. You may not like them, but you need to know."

"Great," I said, sarcastically.

"I'm sorry, Philip, but the way we both feel right now, we probably should get together on this as soon as possible."

"OK. Tomorrow for dinner for sure. I'll clear the decks and check with Earl."

"Good."

"Margo?"

"Hm?"

"Are we through?"

"You mean through talking?"

"No, I mean finished through."

"I don't know. Maybe."

That wasn't what I wanted, or expected, to hear. I knew she was having problems with our relationship, but I had been hoping she would say it had just been a phase, a stage, a mood. I didn't understand how she could so casually say that maybe we were through.

I hung up uneasily and with a sense of dread. Not much earlier I had almost wished I were free of the engagement with Margo that had begun so beautifully and now seemed to be ending in frustration. I had thought I wanted to be available to pursue Allyson, but as I headed toward the table I realized the folly of that. I didn't even know her. Besides a little of her sad history, I knew nothing about the girl except that she had a seemingly precious personality, looked people in the eye when she talked to them, and was a beautiful, beautiful lady who had the ability to hide the fact that she knew it—if indeed she did.

"Sorry," I said as I sat down.

"Did you break your date with Margo smoothly?" Allyson asked.

"Oh, no, it wasn't really a date," I said, not quite lying. "We were just going to talk about something."

"A case?"

"Something like that."

Earl stiffened. My evasiveness surprised him. He couldn't imagine that I would be hiding my engagement to Margo from anyone, even if it *was* on the skids. I couldn't imagine it either, but that didn't stop me. I knew it was foolish, but when Allyson innocently forced the issue, I rationalized a half truth I would live to regret.

"I got the impression that you and Margo might have something going together," she tried.

"No, uh-uh," I said. "Not really. No."

Earl's face was buried in his menu, but his eyes burned accusingly at me from over the top.

Chapter Seven

Earl decidedly froze me out during the small talk before ordering, ignoring every attempt by Allyson to bring me into the conversation. I couldn't blame him. He could have just called my bluff, told Allyson that Margo and I had been engaged for months and in love for a lot longer than that, but he was going to let me stew in my own juices.

When our salads were delivered, Allyson bowed her head slightly, closed her eyes, and appeared to be praying for a few seconds. I couldn't believe it. I don't think Earl even noticed. I had to ask her.

"Do you mind if I ask why you did that?"

"Did what?"

"Appeared to be praying there?"

"I was. I always pray before I eat."

"Why?"

"Well, Philip, it would take a while to explain. Maybe we can talk about it sometime."

"No, I know why you did it. It's because you know that God is the source of our provisions, and so you thank Him for them before you eat. Right?"

"Right."

Earl saw his opportunity to nail me without blowing my cover on the relationship I was hiding. "You believe that too, don't you, Philip?"

"Yes, I do, and so that's why I was wondering, Allyson, if you were—"

"Then why," Earl interrupted, "don't *you* pray before you eat?"

"I usually do," I said.

"Not around me you don't," he said.

"Well, I don't want to offend you. I know that you don't share my view about God, and—"

"I certainly share your view that God is our provider. Most sane people know that. I just don't buy your gung-ho, prosyletizing, drag everybody and his brother into the kingdom ideas."

I was hurt. "Those aren't my ideas. I just believe that followers of Christ are called to share their faith and—"

"And you believe Christ is the only way to God."

"Right."

"Well, I don't," Earl said.

"I do," Allyson said kindly.

Earl nodded that that was all right with him, but I couldn't leave it alone.

"You do?" I said, a little too loudly. "I mean, you're a Christian, not just religious?"

"Yes," she said. "My mother had hardly ever taken me to her Catholic church, but when I was overseas from nineteen seventy until nineteen seventy-two when I graduated from high school, I got in with a group of kids who introduced me to Christ."

"Grief," Earl said, smiling for Allyson, but dead serious for me. "I'm surrounded by 'em."

"My mother didn't like it too much when I wrote her about it. For a while she even hinted that she was going to bring me home, but I think she eventually sensed a change in me, even through my letters."

"How does she feel about it now?" I said.

"She's become a Christian. She started going to church with me in the mid-seventies and now we're in this thing together, as they say."

"Margo's a Christian too," Earl said, staring at me. "Christians stick together, right?" He was really twisting the knife.

"I sense you aren't too open to the idea yourself, Mr. Haymeyer," Allyson said. "Am I right?"

"I wouldn't say I was closed to it," Earl said. "But I do like to separate business and religion, and I have had the whole pitch from Philip here, sometimes even on company time."

"I wouldn't mind trying to change your mind about aggressive Christians someday," Allyson said. "I think people can be told about Christ without being forced into the church. I might even pay two ninety a day for the privilege of telling you on work time."

"For two ninety a day I'll listen to anything," Earl said, and we all laughed. But when he caught my eye, his smile died. Misrepresenting my feelings for Margo was bad enough for me, not to mention Margo. But for what it was doing to my example before Earl, I was ashamed. What could I say? What could I do to make it right?

"Anyway, Philip," Allyson was saying, "it's great to know I have a brother working for me."

"Yeah," I said, less than enthusiastically. I was cringing under the heat of Earl's eyes.

When we had finished eating, Earl asked if we could get back to business.

"Sure," Allyson said, reaching for her fashionably large leather purse. She pulled out a half-inch-thick manila folder as Earl produced a mini tape recorder and placed it near her.

"I waited three years for the chance to see what had been in that first shoe box," she said. "It wasn't until after I returned from high school and was allowed to stay overnight at his apartment that I got it. I was taking a huge risk, I know, but when he was in the bathroom in the morning, I hurried into his bedroom, dropped to all fours, and dug around under the bed for the shoeboxes. The first one had the cash and stuff in it. I shoved it back underneath. I pulled a big rubber band off the other and dumped its contents into my overnight bag, being careful not to let the stuff fall out of order. I was nervous the rest of the time that weekend, worrying that Father would discover that everything was missing from the box. Saturday evening I told him I had an errand to run, and I went to the public library and spent a lot of money photocopying everything from the box. I copied fronts and backs of pictures and every document. The next morning I replaced the contents in the same order I had taken them, but I broke the rubber band on the box. I tied it together and put the knot on the bottom, then dove back out into the other room when I heard Father leaving the bathroom. I don't know to this day if he ever noticed."

"And what you have in this folder are the photocopies of what you found in the box?" Earl said.

"That's right, but I have a few questions first."

"That's fine," Earl said, "and I want you to know that we are not interested in the photocopies."

Both Allyson and I snapped our heads up. "Why not?"

"They could be extremely valuable to us in investigating whatever it is you want investigated, Allyson, but until I know what that is, I wouldn't touch them. And if you should ever want to see your father prosecuted because of anything you found in the box, you'd have a tough time because of how the material was obtained."

"Why would I want to have him prosecuted?"

"I don't know. *Do* you?"

"No, but that's the whole point. If you find something in the course of your investigation—let's say you're just helping me discover his parents, even if it means in some German cemetery somewhere—and you run across a crime he committed. Are you bound to expose him for that?"

"Not necessarily, Allyson," Earl said. "It depends on the crime committed, where, and how long ago."

"Can I ask you a little more specifically without incriminating him?"

"Sure. I won't pursue any line of questioning unless you tell me more than you want to."

"Let me ask this way, and you tell me if I'm treading on dangerous ground. Hypothetically, referring to any such crime or any such criminal, is there a time limit as to how soon a murderer has to be caught before he can be prosecuted?"

"You mean is there a statute of limitations on murder?"

"Yeah."

"No."

"Just curious. And is there a statute of—what did you call it?"

"Limitations."

"Yes, is there a statue of limitations on war crimes?"

"That depends on the war and the crime. Most of the war crimes committed in this century are beyond prosecution, but of course the war crimes of the Nazis in World War Two are still open cases. Nazis have been found in this country and elsewhere ever since the Nuremburg trials, and the perpetrators are still tried, often convicted, and sentenced." Earl was abruptly quiet.

A pall had fallen over the evening. I stared at Allyson, unable to speak. The waitress came by and asked if anyone wanted dessert. We all shook our heads. Allyson put the folder back in her purse. Earl put the recorder in his suitcoat pocket and flapped his credit card down onto the check. We sat in uneasy silence until the waitress picked it up and Earl was able to direct his energy toward small talk with her.

I helped Allyson with her coat on the way out, she

thanked me and then Earl for opening the door for her, and that was the extent of our conversation until we arrived back at the office.

"That's my car right there," she told Earl.

He pulled next to it and shifted into Park. "Allyson," he said, "the preliminary interview is always free, no matter how long it lasts. The way it stands now, you had a nice chat with a couple of friends. If you want to contract for our services, you know the terms. I would need to know only precisely what it is you would like to have us find out, and we would do everything we could to find it out. Let me just add this: if you have any reason to believe about your father what you intimated tonight, I would not hire private investigators—at least law-abiding ones—to check out any part of his background. The study of a childhood in an orphanage or the tracing of long-since-dead parents could lead to areas you want left undetected. The atrocities of World War Two are history. The man you know as your father seems gentle and harmless, though tormented by something in his past. If you don't want to be responsible for what could happen to him after more than thirty years of hard work in this country, I would leave the whole thing alone. Do you understand what I'm saying to you?"

"Yes, I'm afraid I do," Allyson said, her voice trembling as I had not heard it all day. "But if my curiosity gets the better of me, and I just have to know?"

"My offer stands," Earl said. "My only fear is that if we find something you don't want to know, you may wind up having hired us and being our enemy all at the same time."

She reached a hand across to Earl and shook his. "Thank you, Mr. Haymeyer. I appreciate your counsel." She reached back to me. I took her hand warmly. "And thank you, Philip. I imagine I'll see you both around." She left the car and trotted to hers.

Earl removed the mini tape recorder from his suitcoat and turned it off.

We sat in his car until she drove away, then went up into the office. "It never even crossed my mind that her father might have been a Nazi," Earl said. "I hate to admit it, but I never thought of it until she mentioned it. I suppose I should have, figuring her age and the age her father would be. He would have been in Nazi Germany as a young man, military age or so, at the time of Hitler."

"Is it true that if those facts came out about him in the course of a routine investigation, you would have to turn him in?"

"That or face charges of protecting a war criminal, which could be regarded as treasonous."

"And how about your advising her that she should leave it alone if she suspects that? Would that not be regarded the same?"

"I don't think so," Earl said. "I have it on tape just in case. I was—in my opinion—advising a family member, who would not be required to testify against her father anyway. If she was the only one who knew or suspected, he would never face charges."

"Do you feel you should go to the authorities with what you heard tonight?"

"I didn't hear anything tonight, Philip. And neither did you."

Chapter Eight

"You know how my conscience is, Earl," I said. "Please tell me that I shouldn't feel guilty about keeping her suspicions quiet."

"Philip, think about it. She gave us nothing. A German immigrant has nightmares, and she wonders if war crimes have a statute of limitations. There is nothing there to share with anyone. If you have a conscience, my boy, it oughta be working overtime right now anyway, wouldn't you say?"

"I suppose. You were pretty hard on me, ya know."

"You deserved it."

"I know." And that was true. I knew I had to pray about it, but, frankly, I was afraid of how God might lead.

"What's going on, Philip? Can't you and Margo have a few serious discussions about your relationship, maybe even a few quarrels, without you turning on her and then jumping ship?"

"That's not it, Earl. I just don't see why I should get in the way of any potential I might have with Allyson by telling her I'm engaged, especially if my fiancée wants to end the engagement. You never heard me deny my love for Margo before."

"True enough, but you sure seem eager to get it over with now. I thought Margo's breaking it off would be harder on you."

"Allyson could make it easier."

"Get off it. First, it takes an incredible ego to think you could get to first base with a girl like that. Face it, pal, if Margo hadn't had big troubles and been attracted to your chivalry, you probably wouldn't have gotten anything going with her, either."

I couldn't believe I was hearing this from Earl. What was he saying? I never claimed to be much to look at or listen to, but why should I feel like a second-class citizen? Earl could tell he had as good as punched me in the stomach.

"Don't take it so hard, Philip. All I'm trying to say is that you'd better not get your hopes up on Allyson Scheel. She's a classy young lady, an international traveler, smart as a whip. She's got money, she's got security."

"But she needs me."

"Whatdya mean? All you two have in common is that you pray before meals, and *you* don't even do that half the time. It'll take more than religion to start anything smoldering with her."

"How many times do I hafta tell you it's not religion?" I said.

"And how many times do I have to tell you that it's only you and your religious friends who say it's not religion? Everyone else says you're religious and that you've got religion, so no matter what you say about it

74

being a person or a relationship or a way of life or whatever else you call it, to most people that's religion. You act as if there's something wrong with religion so you'd like to pretend that faith in God or Christ or the church is something other than religion."

"It's better than religion. Religion is a trap, confining. Christ is freedom."

"So you're better than everyone else."

"I didn't say—"

"You're even better than other religious people, because they call their religion religion, but to you it's a trap. Don't you see that that's what stands in the way of people buying your package, Philip? You are one of the nicest kids I know. Except for a few occasional incidents of inconsistency, which heaven knows I can't criticize people for, I think the world of you. But your religion— excuse me—your faith would be less offensive if it was more live-and-let-live."

"But one of the major tenets of Christianity is that it is evangelical," I said. "I don't want to badger you, to drag you to Christ. I just want the right to tell you about Him, to share with you what He has to offer. That's all. No obligation. I can't make you buy it. You can reject it. But don't deny me the right to tell you about it."

"I never have, Philip. I've even given you time to tell the whole staff. All I'm saying is that you had better have your own life in order, and you'd better be careful about your better-than-everyone-else attitude before you start the pitch."

He had me, and I knew it. You don't sell even the best

product on the market with a we-don't-need-you-you-need-us attitude. I pursed my lips and nodded. Message received, loud and clear.

"And like I say, Philip. Don't take it too hard. I want to see you mellow out a little, but don't think I'd want you without your relig—your, uh, faith. I want you pretty much just the way you are. If there is any truth to all this, I'm gonna need you around."

I forced a smile. He *was* well-intentioned. And worst of all, he acted like more of a Christian than I did in many ways. He was honest, forthright, compassionate. Right then I felt the opposite.

Earl was tidying up the office, and I was switching off lights. "Whadya think, Philip?" he asked. "Is Allyson going to be back asking for our help?"

"I don't know. I guess if she just can't stand the tension she will. I'm intrigued by this idea that he's going somewhere, but not to Germany. Where could he be going? If she's even close with her fear about his past, he'd be pretty brave to travel far internationally, wouldn't he?"

"Good thinking. If you really are going to try to see her again, let me know if she finds out where he's going. I'd like to help her, if we can. Hey, here's a note from Shipman. He was here! What time is it?"

"Quarter to eleven. Why?"

"It says to call him if I'm back before ten thirty. I think I'm gonna try him. I want to know what he found out for Bonnie today. Get me his home number from her file and then listen in on the extension."

I did better than that. I peeled off my coat and tossed it over Bonnie's chair, found Larry's number, and dialed it from her switchboard. When it was ringing, I buzzed Earl.

Shipman answered groggily. "Hello?"

"Boy, when you say ten thirty, you mean ten thirty, don't you?"

"Oh, hi, Earl. Yeah, I guess. I was sleepin'."

"You wanna talk, Ship, or you wanna go back to sleep and call me in the morning?"

"Naw, I'm awright. Let's talk. I spent some time at the son-in-law's office today, nosing around. It's weird, but the scuttlebutt in the office is that this Carla can hardly stand to be around Greg. Everybody knows they were engaged years ago, and the way they play it at work is that they aren't even on speaking terms. If they're faking it, they're good at it. She tries to nail him at every turn. She forgets to give him important phone messages, leaves his name off the routing slips on memos from the boss, embarrasses him, and is openly hostile. He tries to be nice, but it appears she's out to get him."

"I wasn't expecting *that,* Ship. How long has it been going on? Wasn't she partly responsible for getting him hired?"

"No, if you can believe the flunkies in the office. The word is that she opposed it from the beginning and had to be sweet-talked into it by the boss. He made her promise to make the best of it, pledged to keep them apart, and all that. She really resents having to go along on luncheons when he's involved."

77

"Hey, Lar," Earl said slowly. "How'd you get all this dope?"

"Oh, uh, I was sorta the, uh, copy machine repairman today. Amazing what a charming supplier can get out of the secretaries if he's friendly and speaks generically about the strange office he just visited. I told a girl there that one of my clients has all kinds of scandal in the office. 'I don't suppose you have any of that kind of excitement around here,' I suggested. Before you knew it, it all came out: the best potential for scandal. A single woman works with her former fiancée, who is now married. But it's *not* a scandal. She seems to hate him. Hard to know if it's true or just a sham, but if it's a game, he's being hurt by it."

"You know I don't like us to misrepresent ourselves, Ship," Earl said.

"I know, chief, but what did you want me to do, announce that I'm a private investigator looking for facts about the Greg and Carla affair for Greg's mother-in-law?"

I laughed.

"Is that you, Philip?" Shipman said.

"Yeah. How ya doin'?"

"Fine, but, Earl, you gotta tell me when Holy Joe is listenin' in so I don't make some wisecrack about God or whatever."

"He can take it," Earl said. "Thanks for the information, and get back to bed."

"I am in bed—I'm just not asleep. Or maybe I am. Anyway, that's not all I've got."

"It isn't?"

"No, and I'm not sure Bonnie's gonna want to know what else there is."

"What're you saying?"

"First tell me Bonnie's not listening in, too."

"It's just the two of us, Ship. Now what'd you get?"

"Well, after I got what I wanted from Greg's office, I drove over to his and Linda's apartment. I don't know what I expected to find, but my timing was perfect. Remember the guy, good-looking, about forty, who went to lunch with Greg and the boss and Carla and the other woman?"

"Yeah."

"I saw his sports car parked at the apartment building."

"What time was this?"

"About 1:30 in the afternoon."

"OK—"

"So I put on my painter's hat and coveralls and grabbed a can and hung around the hallway near Greg and Linda's apartment, always within view of their door. I don't know how long he had been there before I got there, but he came out of their apartment at three twenty, exactly ten minutes before Erin, the thirteen-year-old, arrived home from school."

"Who is this guy?"

"Name's Johnny Bizell. A friend of mine in the sixteenth precinct ran a ten twenty-eight on the license number for me."

"That's the worst news I've heard all day, Ship.

Thanks a lot."

"You know Bizell?"

"No, but the thought that Linda is covering her own garbage with stories about her husband is going to kill Bonnie. I wish I was working for *his* mother instead."

"I'm going to stay on it, Earl. I want to be sure before you tell Bonnie anything. Good night, boys."

Earl and I gathered up our stuff and trudged down the hall to our respective apartments. There was nothing to say, but Earl said it anyway as he stopped to unlock his door. "I didn't need this tonight," he said.

"I know what you mean. Hey, Earl, I need to have dinner with Margo tomorrow night. Can I avoid overtime?"

"I think so, unless we get another Allyson-style walk-in. I want to see things work out for you and Margo, you know."

"I know. I appreciate it."

"You don't sound too optimistic about it, Philip."

"I'm not."

Chapter Nine

I didn't sleep well. I knew I should be planning what to say to Margo the next evening, but after all, it was her party, not mine. As far as I was concerned, as long as she wanted to continue our engagement and build toward marriage, I certainly did, too. It was only lately, when she quit wearing her diamond and hinted that she wanted out, that I became resentful.

I'm sure I would not have considered any potential with Allyson Scheel had Margo not been in her present state of mind. I had always enjoyed watching Allyson, sure, but so had everyone else in the office. I had never had roving eyes for anyone. But now, when I should have been planning strategy or trying to figure what was making Margo tick or what it would take to convince her that we were right for each other, all I could think of was Allyson.

I felt guilty about it, and disloyal. Even fickle. I lay on my back with my hands behind my head, staring at a ceiling I could hardly see in the darkness, reliving the past few hours. Most of the conversation had been between Allyson and Earl, but I had caught her eyes a few times. We were communicating. We shared moments. When Earl said something funny, she threw her head back and laughed and looked at me.

God was nudging my conscience. I ran from the feeling and continued to dwell on Allyson. She wasn't afraid to be a kindred spirit. And when she was talking or listening to me, she looked me full in the face. That's flattering, no matter who does it. But when it is someone who is simply so exciting just to look at—

I knew there was nothing to it yet, and that she would have no idea what I was thinking. I was not so immature that I would think she was excited by me the way I was about her. And I also knew that if she *was* made aware of my interest, she would have been surprised. She was obviously an old-fashioned girl, practical to the point where she wouldn't put much stock in the heartthrobs of someone who had seen her around and had spent a few hours with her.

Anyway, I knew Earl had a point, though a painful one. Here was a girl out of my class. Of course, that had never stopped me before. Margo had been full of pain and problems, yet compared to me, she had been raised as a rich girl, cultured, exposed to the finer things of life. That was not intimidating to me. In fact, I had learned a lot from her. She always said I was better for her than she was for me, but even my social graces, graceless as they were, had been revolutionized by observing her in public.

Allyson had that same air about her, and I was glad that I had learned from Margo to be calm and collected and matter-of-fact in social settings. Good grief, I was using things I had learned from my fiancée to try to make a good impression—or at least to avoid making a bad impression—on a new woman.

A new woman. Wouldn't that be nice? Not that I had grown tired of Margo. But if she wanted out, what was I supposed to do? This was no old movie where the star pines away, remains true to his rejecting love, and wins her back in the end because of his persistence. Margo wasn't the type who would consciously want me to work at keeping her. If she wanted a break, I would give it to her, and I wouldn't penalize myself by waiting for her and pretending that I still was a one-girl guy.

I was rationalizing, and I knew it. But the guilt wasn't as strong as the desire.

I rolled onto my side and pulled the ends of the pillow up around my ears. I stared at the red digits on my clock radio and watched them change to 2:17. I shut my eyes hard and commanded myself to sleep. The next morning the staff would meet for its weekly session. Several cases were in the works, and Shipman would report on the Greg and Linda affair, uh, matter. Bonnie would not likely be allowed to attend.

I always looked forward to those meetings because the new assignments were made, and Earl was at his best, making suggestions, offering tips and reminders. Since the A. SCHEEL case was obviously not going to take me overseas, I wondered what else he would have in store for me. The fact that he would even consider me for such a plum and the bonus it involved (Earl always shares the additional income on unusual cases with the investigator) encouraged me. I knew he was happy with my work, and I wanted to show him that I could be trusted with anything he thought I was ready for.

I needed to sleep to be at my best. The next time I looked at the clock, an hour had passed. I turned to a classical music FM station, thought a little about Margo and a lot about Allyson, and finally fell asleep.

It seemed I hadn't seen Larry Shipman for days. In fact, I hadn't. Our cases, seldom calling for us to work together, had scrambled our schedules to the point where he was in the office when I was out, and vice versa. That was another advantage of the weekly staff meetings.

"Mornin', good-lookin'," he said, giving Margo a brotherly squeeze when she arrived.

"Hi, Lar," she said. "Who's on the desk over lunch today?"

"Believe you are, kid," he told her.

"Wonderful."

"I know you love it. Where's the chief?"

Bonnie could hear us from the switchboard. "He'll be here any minute," she said. "I'm not joining you this morning. Hope that means good news."

"Hope so," Margo echoed.

Larry and I already knew differently.

"Want Philip and I to bring you something back from lunch today, Margo?" Larry asked.

"Yeah, thanks. Where you going?"

"I dunno," he said. "Where do you wanna go, Philip? Or maybe I should ask Margo where she wants us to go. I'm not particular."

"I might not be able to go with you," I said. "I'll let you know mid-morning."

"Something going with the boss, huh, Ambitious?" Larry said, jabbing me on the shoulder.

"Naw."

"Then he's cheatin' on you, Margo! I just knew it!"

When neither of us laughed or looked at each other or even at him, Larry stage-whispered, "Whoops! Not the day for that line, huh? Sorry, kids! Anyway, Margo, I'll check with you before lunch to see what you want."

Earl, looking grim, drew the door shut behind him, greeted everyone a bit more formally than usual, and quickly turned on the tape recorder. "We've all got a lot of work to do, so let's get rolling. How is everybody?"

We all responded with some form of signal. Margo shrugged. I stuck out one hand, palm down, and tipped it back and forth. Larry signaled thumbs up, but added, "Except for what I found yesterday."

"Oh, no," Margo said. "Was Bonnie right? Was Linda right?"

"Worse than that," Larry said, waiting for Earl's cue and then telling her the whole story.

"That's terrible," she decided. "What next, Earl? How do you deal with that, finding the opposite of what you were looking for?"

"You just keep looking," he said, "until you know all you want or need to know. Then you tell the client as gently and as forthrightly as you can, and let her do what she wants."

"But Earl," Larry said, "what do I say to the client

this morning when she asks what I saw yesterday?"

"Use your imagination. I'm telling you that you can't talk yet about what you saw, because nothing's been confirmed yet. And you know that's true."

"Yeah, but you know as well as I do that it looks pretty bad for Linda to have a man in her apartment all afternoon, leaving just before the daughter gets home."

"Still, Ship," Earl said, "what *are* you going to tell Bonnie, based on what I just told you?"

"You don't want me to tell her anything now, yet you don't want me to appear evasive?"

"You got it."

"I'll think about it."

"Margo," Earl said, "tell us where things stand on your case."

Margo sounded tired, but her thoughts were clear and she represented herself well, as usual. "I've traced a major part of the drug supply at Glencoe High School to a history teacher, a Mrs. Millicent."

"A married lady?" Shipman said.

"No longer married, and hardly a lady, I'm afraid," Margo said. "She puts on a good front, doesn't appear to be any less than the model mid-thirties, with-it teacher. But too much points her way."

"Should we inform the drug prevention boys at the Metropolitan Enforcement Group?" Earl asked. "The school board liaison just wanted a good lead before going to the police, and my guess is that we've used up their budget for this. How long have you been on it now?"

Margo checked her file. "Today will be thirteen days."

"They allotted five thousand dollars," Earl said, studying his client registration sheet. "That gives you four more days if you have a plan. What will you do, or should we just give 'em what we've got?"

"I want to go in there," Margo said. "I want to be a transfer student from anywhere, and I want to get next to Mrs. M."

"Not a bad idea, but can you pass for an eighteen-year-old, and can you look hungry for drugs within four days of meeting her without scaring her off?"

"I could pass for *sixteen,* unfortunately," Margo said. "As for the four days, probably not. But if they want this woman nailed in the act of selling, they're gonna need me."

"But a police undercover agent would be cheaper. In fact, free," Earl countered.

"Yeah," Larry interrupted, "but those kids know every stinkin' one of 'em."

"That's right," Margo said. "I'd say it would be worth asking the board for a little extension, say another ten days. Could we maybe give them a price break?"

"For what?" Earl said. "Volume?" We laughed. "I'll just tell them we need ten more days. If they want a break on the price, let 'em ask for it. I'm sure not going to hand it out unless they ask."

"They'll ask," Larry said.

"And I'll probably relent," Earl said. "This is one case I'd like to see through to the end. Get her, Margo. It's bad enough kids are getting drugs from the sleaze on the streets without having to see this kind of an example at school. I'll grease the wheels for your transfer. Where do you want to be from?"

"Better make it Atlanta," she said. "It's the only place I can talk about intelligently other than Winnetka, and there would be too many people with friends in Winnetka who haven't seen me in high school lately."

Earl coached Margo on how to keep a low profile while getting next to the teacher and casually getting on the subject of liberal views of freedom, and so on. It made me wish I was in on it, and I knew Margo would do a good job.

"Now, Dr. Spence," Earl said expansively. "Even though you've been in my doghouse a bit lately on peripheral matters"—Larry looked puzzled; Margo didn't—"I must congratulate you in the presence of your peers for your outstanding work on the Ussry missing person report. As the rest of you probably remember, the police didn't want to touch the case of Mr. Ussry's missing son because there had been some contact made through friends, indicating that the boy—what was his name, Philip? Right, Frank—was happy and healthy but that he had no interest in reestablishing any relationship with the family. As he was eighteen, there was really nothing the police could do, and Mr. Ussry, being a man of some means, contacted us. According to Philip's report"—he dug out the copy Bonnie had typed the day before—"within eight days Philip was able to locate the boy in Cleveland, visit him, negotiate a meeting between father and son, and completely satisfy the client. Excellent work."

"I can't say the boy will be coming home," I said. "In fact, he won't be. But he was able to explain to his father his reasons for feeling he had to leave. He refused any financial support and insists on making it on his own. He prefers that his father not try to contact him anymore, but Frank promised to keep him posted on his well-being. I think it will be all right in the end."

"Well, it was a fine piece of work, Philip. You're progressing well, and I hope you can tell how pleased I am. We don't have time this meeting, but on your own, Margo and Larry, I want you to read this report and see how Philip found the boy and what he said to both parties to start the healing process. Sometimes our work involves more than just sleuthing. There's compassion and psychology involved."

"Thanks, Earl," I said, feeling less high than I thought I should after such a compliment.

"Now," he said, "I want to bounce Allyson Scheel's story off the two of you who haven't heard it yet."

"The Allyson Scheel from downstairs?" Shipman said, leaning forward in his chair.

Earl nodded.

"I'm all ears. And eyes."

Chapter Ten

Earl played selected portions of the tapes he had made the night before. "What do you hear that I'm not hearing?" he asked after an hour.

"Well, my guess is that she won't be back, chief," Larry said. "Are you sure you want to spend the time on it?"

Before Earl could answer, Margo cut in. "You're wrong. She'll be back. She loves her father, and she wants to know, she *has* to know about his past. It's not just curiosity. She cares. She wants to help. Earl, you should have told her that she can't testify against her own father, even if he *was* a Nazi. And you can't use any of the solid stuff she gives you if it came from a shoebox she obtained illegally. I don't know how she's going to help him if he was a Nazi, but maybe she can find a way to help him deal with his guilt."

"Well, as long as we're going to talk about it," Shipman said, "I did hear something. According to what she said, her father never told her he was going to Germany."

"Whadya mean?" I said. "He told her several times he was going to his homeland, and he said he was raised

91

in Germany in an orphanage. He also showed her the box of savings toward the trip."

"She saw a brochure from a travel agency, but she didn't say for what country," Larry said. "And he never *said* Germany."

"I think it was just the way she repeated the story, Larry," Earl said. "But let's keep it in mind. The man has a German accent, but he has never talked much about his past."

"I say he was born somewhere else before being sent to the orphanage in Germany by officials, church people, distant relatives, or someone," Larry continued. "He probably knows of that country and wants to go there either to trace his family or to claim it as his homeland, as he says."

The rest of us looked dubious, but I was intrigued. It always amazes me what others hear in conversations that I don't.

"I've got a few potential cases I want to go over with you, Philip," Earl said. "Meanwhile, Margo will stay on the school board assignment; Ship, you hang in with Greg and Linda; and I'll try to stay available if Allyson Scheel returns. That's all for now."

It was nearly lunchtime, and as we headed back to our desks, I heard one of Shipman's all time great lines. Bonnie asked him what he had learned about her son-in-law the day before. "Nothing to speak of yet, Bon," he said. "Nothing to speak of."

Bonnie, Earl, and Larry quickly organized to go out for lunch together and took Margo's order as she got situated at the switchboard. "I'll see you tonight," I said softly. She nodded.

As I left I heard Larry asking her, "Where's the rock today?"

"Home," she said, as noncommitally as possible.

I bounded down the stairs and out the door, strode up the sidewalk to the other end of the building, and ducked into the Beatrice Boutique, not realizing that I was out of breath. "May I help you, sir?" a salesgirl asked.

"No, uh, yeah, I'd like to see Allyson."

"May I tell her who's calling?"

"Sure."

"Your name?"

"Oh, yeah, Philip. Philip from upstairs. No, don't tell her from upstairs. She'll know."

I didn't want her mother to know she was seeing anyone from the detective agency in case Allyson hadn't told her anything about her plans.

The girl returned. "Allyson asked if I would tell you that she is still thinking about it and will call you." She started to walk away.

"Thanks," I said, "but that isn't what I wanted to see her about. Could you ask her if I could talk to her for just a second?" She hesitated, then went back to the office again. I smiled when Allyson appeared, but she didn't flash her usual response.

"Hi, Philip. Listen, my mother doesn't know I've talked to you and Mr. Haymeyer, and I'd just as soon keep it that way until I decide what I'm going to do. I appreciate your interest, but I got the impression from your boss last night that he thought maybe I shouldn't pursue this. Does he know you're checking with me again right away?"

I held up both hands to try to get her attention, and she finally gave me an opening. "I'm not here on business," I said. "We never try to talk people into retaining us, anyway. It's unprofessional, and it doesn't work. You would prove that all over again. Anyway, we have plenty of work. I'm here to see you."

She smiled but said nothing.

"I was wondering if you were free for lunch."

"Well, I usually just run down the street here for a sandwich. I don't take much time to eat because I like to get back and help Mother with the books and all. One of our clients is coming in today who orders her spring wardrobe about now each year, and she will not talk with anyone except Mother and me."

"I would enjoy taking you to lunch, Allyson," I said, finally having caught my breath. "We can go to your usual spot, or you can go with me to one of my usual places, and I promise to have you back here whenever you say."

She cocked her head and gave me a pretty, closed-mouth smile. "Fair enough," she said. "If we leave now, which is a little earlier than usual for me, I can take an hour."

"Great, that'll give me time to take you to a neat Italian place I think you'll like. You do like Italian food?"

"Love it. Let me get my coat."

As we walked to my car, I purposely slowed her down to make sure that my three co-workers would be gone by the time we rounded the corner. They were, but I realized as I opened the door for her and then went around to my side that Margo would have a perfect view of us from one of the office windows if she chose to look, as I did nearly everyday. I didn't dare look up to see.

Allyson smiled a lot and talked a little. While we waited for our food, I asked if I could talk business just for a minute. "It's not really business, because I really do care after hearing your story last night. Whether we take the case or not."

"It's OK, Philip," she said.

"It's just that one of our guys, Larry Shipman, noticed that your father never told you he was going to Germany, so maybe you shouldn't be so surprised that he isn't booked on a flight to there."

She thought for a moment. "He's right. Father never did say Germany. I just assumed—"

"So did I," I said. "So did Earl."

"So my next step is to find out where he's going, even if I don't retain your firm."

"Yeah, and I'd be curious to know when you find out. Just curious for my own sake, I mean."

"I appreciate that, Philip. Sure. I'll tell you if I find out."

"Thanks. Enough business for today?"

"Yeah. Hey, you know a lot about me because of last night. How 'bout telling me about you?"

"There's not much to tell," I said, but I told her anyway.

"Do you miss illustration work, now that you're out of it fulltime?" she said in the car on the way back.

"Not really. I still draw on my own time now and then, but I regret not having gotten into detective work earlier. Of course, then I probably wouldn't have had the chance to learn the trade under Earl. He's the best, you know."

"I sensed that. Are you talking business again, selling me on him?" She was smiling.

"No. I say that even to people who aren't prospective clients."

"I believe you do," she said.

I dropped her off in front of the boutique. "Thank you very much for lunch, Philip," she said, her eyes locked on mine. "It was a good idea, a good place, and I enjoyed the company."

"My pleasure," I said, as if I had just delivered her paper.

"Thank you," she said, almost shyly. " 'Bye."

I was high at work that afternoon, but something was eating at me, too. I had told her about how I met Margo and that bringing her to Chicago and helping expose her mother as a murderer had led us both into detective work. But I never even hinted that Margo and I had fallen in love and were engaged. Of course, maybe after tonight we wouldn't be engaged, but I could have just told Allyson that. She wouldn't have thought it improper for me to be taking her to lunch when my fiancée had quit wearing her engagement ring. I think.

But I didn't want her to think for a moment that I was

showing interest in her because I was on the rebound from a disappointment. Because of Allyson, the disappointment I probably would have felt over Margo was dispelled somewhat. I knew that was rotten, but it was the truth. Maybe Margo was right. Maybe we were taking each other for granted and were tired of each other. That wasn't exactly what she had been saying, but with an exciting newcomer in my world, maybe Margo *was* beginning to seem routine.

I didn't think I would have felt that way if Margo had still been excited about me, about us, about our future, but I couldn't be sure. Something had pulled the plug on her feelings for me, and it was hard to take. I didn't want to force anything, so maybe I should just let it happen. We could still be friends. In fact, we'd always be more than friends. We had been through so much, and she had received Christ. We were family. We didn't have to be in love.

I told Earl about my conversation with Allyson without telling him I had taken her to lunch. I knew I wouldn't be able to hide it long if I continued to see her, not with all of us together in one big, happy building.

"Unless her father is going somewhere really unusual, I doubt we'll ever hear from Allyson again," Earl predicted.

Well, we might not, I thought, *but I will.*

"Take a look at these two folders this afternoon, and let's talk tomorrow morning about them," Earl said. "We've got to get you back into circulation soon, don't we?"

"Yeah. Listen, Earl, do you mind if I take the

afternoon off and get some sleep? I didn't sleep well last night, and you know I've got that important dinner with Allyson, I mean Margo, tonight. I'll read the case files late tonight and be ready for tomorrow morning, OK?"

"Sure."

Chapter Eleven

I told Margo what I was doing and asked if she would mind calling me when she left work so I could get up and get ready. For some reason, because of the strain between us, I felt uneasy asking such a favor, and I sensed she felt the same, though it was the type of thing we had done for each other without question before.

When my phone rang at 5:30, I assumed it was Margo, but it wasn't.

"Can I talk with you tonight, Philip?" Allyson said.

"Sure, what about?"

"Business," she said. "I'm still not sure I want to retain EH, but I just have to show someone what I found in the shoebox. Can I do it off the record just to see what you think? I found out where Father is going by asking a friend in a travel agency in Evanston to check my father's name through all the airline companies."

"Where's he going?"

"I'd rather tell you in person, Philip, if you don't mind. And I want to show you the photocopies of the contents of the box first anyway. Is that OK?"

"Sure. When?"

"Soon?"

"Oh, I can't, Allyson. Ya know I was supposed to have a meeting with Margo last night, and I canceled. I just can't cancel tonight."

"How about later? Will your meeting last long?"

"No, I hope not. I mean, I don't think so. Why don't I call you when I'm free, and we can meet somewhere?"

"Fine, and thanks, Philip."

I called Margo to be sure she hadn't been trying to reach me.

"No," she said. "But I was just about to. When should I be ready?"

"Why don't we just go from here?" I said, realizing I sounded a little eager to get on with it.

"OK, but I'm not gonna look like much."

"I thought you said I shouldn't treat this like a date, that I shouldn't spend much money because of your state of mind or something like that?"

"Yeah, you're right. But I do like to look nice when I go out."

"No need. You look fine. We won't go fancy. Where do you want to go?"

"You decide," she said.

"No, it's your deal, really. I mean, it is, isn't it? You know what I mean. Just anywhere you want will be fine."

"Well, I don't want to spend all evening trying to decide where to go. Let's just go somewhere quiet where we can talk and get a decent meal."

"Fine, Margo. You name it."

"Oh, all right. The Italian place."

I gulped. "Well, I, uh—yeah, that's good. Give me a half hour here to get a shower, and I'll come get you."

"Don't dress up, Philip."

"I won't."

I called Earl to tell him of the development with Allyson, but he was still wary. "I don't want to hear anything incriminating about the man unless she's going to hire us, Philip. Remember that."

We talked about the various possibilities until I realized that I had just ten minutes to get ready. I figured I had treated Margo badly enough lately without showing up late, so I showed up with damp hair instead.

She had retained a bit of her humor in spite of her emotional turmoil. "I said not to dress up," she said, "but you didn't have to go overboard."

I hurried through my meal, hoping we could get on with whatever it was Margo wanted to say. She sensed it. "Got another date tonight?"

"Naw. Just something I'm going to check out for Earl if I have time. No rush."

When we finished dessert and the dishes had been cleared, she was finally ready to talk. "Philip, I know I've been unfair to you with the ring business. You were right, I was wrong. There was no excuse for it, and I want you to forgive me."

"No, it's all right," I said. "If you didn't feel right about wearing it, I understand. I just wish you would have said something so I would have known before other people started to notice."

"That's what I mean. That's what I'm sorry about. I

101

can't say I'm sorry that I'm not wearing it. I do miss what we had, but I don't think we have it anymore, and I need time to sort it out."

"I'll buy that we don't have what we had," I said, "but I confess I don't know why. My feelings for you never changed. I was still in love with you, excited about you, eager to marry you. What happened?"

"I don't know, Philip. Now that you see me in one of my confused states where I am down and moody and troubled and uncertain, what does it do to you?"

"It makes me feel rejected, like I deserve better. I know that's selfish and probably unreasonable, but that's the truth. You asked."

"Yes, I asked. Does it make you love me less?"

"No."

She sensed my hesitance. "No?"

"Well, I don't know. I feel I have lost a lot of what I felt for you."

"You see?"

"Well, does that bother you? I mean you're the one who wants to break the engagement, to have a cooling-off period, to think things over."

"Yes, it bothers me. It proves to me that I need more than a husband has to give. I need someone who will love me and stay with me and see me through times like this. You know I had a weird childhood and that I carry scars that even my faith doesn't seem to erase. I need you to stay with me when I'm upset and confused."

"Stay with you, but not be engaged to you? That's what you call staying with you? I loved you. Supporting you, in my eyes, meant loving you and being your fiancé. You're asking a lot for me to stay by you and be your strength while your emotional trauma evidences itself by shutting me out."

"I know. It's too much to ask. I'm being unfair. Just forget it."

"Margo, if I had known at the beginning of this that this was what you wanted, maybe I could have been ready for it. But I felt pitched out like so much cold dishwater, and I was just adjusting to the fact that you wanted no more of me."

"Well, it didn't take you long to mourn my loss, did it? You sound quite over it by now."

"That's not fair. You should be glad I'm not an emotional cripple over it. You might feel responsible."

"An emotional cripple like me, is that what you're getting at?" she said.

"I didn't mean that at all."

We were silent for several minutes. I found it difficult to look at her. Finally, I spoke. "I thought that maybe I could handle it. That we could be friends, better than that, best friends. We have been through so much together. We could be buddies for life. I could watch you find someone new and get married and always be welcome at your home and with your children. You would be interested in my life, too. We'd be examples of a loving brother and sister in Christ."

"That's nice, Philip, but that isn't what we were building. If it can't work out between us, that would be wonderful. But I don't want second best. I want you as my lover and husband and the father of my children."

I was completely thrown. "What am I supposed to make of all this, Margo? You wring me out and hang me up to dry, I deal with it the only way I know how, and now you change your mind on me."

"I haven't changed my mind. I just don't know where I am. I feel we've lost something, and until we get it back, my dreams won't work. Maybe I'm too romantic. Maybe it's unrealistic to think that the warm fuzzy feelings will last over a long engagement."

"Which I agreed to for your sake," I reminded her. "I knew we had fallen in love under very unusual circumstances, and I agreed that we should really be sure. But I was sure. And I thought you were, too, until now. What do you want, Margo? I'll be or think or do anything you want."

"Well, that attitude, for one thing, I do not want. I would much rather be saying that to you and have you advise me on exactly what I should do. Prescribe the medicine, send me to bed, tell me it'll all be all right in the morning."

"But you really don't want that, do you, Margo?"

"I guess not. I want to give you your ring back, take a break for a while, see what happens to me spiritually and emotionally, and then come running back to you when I'm ready and sure."

"And if you do that, how will I know that we won't go through this again?"

"You'll just have to take my word for it. And I'll make you one pledge right now. If I come back to you, ready to take up again where we left off, I'll want to marry you as soon as we can get organized."

I was dumbfounded. "And what should I do in the meantime?"

"Wait for me."

"Wait for you?"

"Yes. Be patient. It may not take as long as you think, but I don't want to make any promises."

"You also don't want to keep any," I said unkindly, accepting the ring from her outstretched hand. "Are you telling me that I should live under the restrictions of an engaged man while enjoying none of the privileges?"

"What are you saying, Philip?"

"That I'm not sure it's fair that I should deprive myself of a normal life—as I might have if I weren't engaged—when for a while, and perhaps permanently, I am not engaged."

"I missed something," she said.

"No, I think *I* missed something."

"Wait, Philip. You're telling me that if you're not engaged, you'd like to play the field a bit, is that it?"

"Maybe."

"*I* won't be doing that."

"That's your prerogative."

"Philip, I thought it would be torturous to break our engagement, and I expected you to tell me you would wait forever for me to come to my senses, which I probably will do. But you're taking it remarkably well and are even eager to get back into the free life."

I felt foolish, as if I had already confessed that I had

taken Allyson out. "And what if I did wait forever for you, and you didn't come back? Then what?"

"Well, I would have let you know at some point that it was completely over."

"So, this is just a trial period, a time for thinking, a cooling-off period, but you'll let me know when it's for real?"

"You make it sound pretty shallow."

"There's a good reason it sounds shallow, Margo."

We were silent again. I paid the check and returned to the table. I looked at my watch.

"Can you leave it this way, Philip?" Margo asked, incredulous. "Could you go and handle your errands for Earl without our resolving anything here tonight?"

"I'm afraid we *have* resolved something," I said. "I get the impression that you're going to play me for the fool, expect me to wait until you're ready for me, and then pull me out of the mothballs and put me on again."

"Philip, I'm shocked. What do you want, full freedom? Surely I couldn't ask for any commitment from you. But it's not going to help my decision-making if you run right out and start dating while I'm trying to sort things out."

"Margo, you're asking too much. I pledged my life and my tomorrows to you, and the ring you just gave back to me was my symbol. If you want to hang it up, even temporarily, that's *your* choice, not mine."

"You're telling me that if I want you to wait for me, I have to keep the ring and keep wearing it? That would make a difference to you, knowing how I feel right now?"

"No, I would not *offer* the ring to you, knowing how you feel."

"And I wouldn't accept it from you, knowing how *you* feel."

"Fine, then. We're through. You know where to find me."

"Terrific, Philip. I can see working at the office is going to be just peachy under the circumstances."

"We owe it to Earl to not let this get in the way of our work."

"Oh, certainly." She was on the edge of tears.

I could hardly believe what I had heard myself saying. Was I doing this just to justify Allyson in my life? *Was* she in my life? Would she be for long?

"Will you at least take me to my car at the office?" she asked.

"Of course."

On the way she broke down and sobbed. I reached to touch her shoulder, but she shrugged my hand away. When we stopped, I said, "I hate to leave you this way."

"Oh, never mind," she managed, opening the door.

I reached in my shirt pocket for Allyson's home number.

Chapter Twelve

"Philip, can you come to my apartment?" Allyson wanted to know.

I hesitated. "I suppose," I said.

"We can meet somewhere else if you wish," she said. "But my mother is already here and—"

"Oh, well, if you're mother is there."

"Philip," she scolded. "I wouldn't invite you to my apartment alone—"

"*I* know."

"You did *not* know."

"You're right," I said. "You threw me. Listen, where is your mother on all this?"

"I told her almost everything so far."

"And I don't like it much," Mrs. Scheel said a few minutes later, after I had found my way past the doorman and the glassy, carpeted labyrinth that led to Allyson's place. "I have made it a practice—in fact, since Allie returned from high school overseas—to let her make her own decisions. I didn't force her to work with me or for me. I live in this building, but on a different floor. She doesn't answer to me."

"But you *do* tell me what you think," Allyson said.

"And would you have it any other way, dear?"

"Of course not. I need your counsel now more than ever. I don't want to do anything that would hurt either you or Father."

The women were a study in family beauty. Beatrice Scheel appeared a spirited, handsome woman with an open, honest face and hair died jet black. Allyson's soft smile and the flowing red hair around her face were invitations to stare. The women looked good together, like they belonged to each other. And they conversed openly, maturely. The mother stood.

"Philip," she said, "Allyson trusts you. She's a good judge of character, and I have implicit confidence in her. I want to tell you exactly how I feel about this whole thing, and then I want you to advise me. Regardless how I feel about it, then it will be up to Allyson whether she decides to follow up on it. We'll all have to live with the consequences."

She moved to a wing chair near the end of the couch where I sat, leaving Allyson in a love seat directly across from me. Mrs. Scheel tucked her legs beneath her, letting her floor-length lounging coat cover her feet. When she was situated, she reached out without looking, and Allyson handed her her saucer and cup of tea as if it had been choreographed. She set it carefully on the arm of the chair and didn't touch it again until she was finished talking.

"I can understand Allie's need to know. I lived with that need for years. I should say I *have* lived with that need. I never outgrew it or got over it. I loved that man. That has dissipated somewhat because I have all but given up on finding the key that unlocks him. I have prayed for him for the last several years, but I have not asked him about his past for more than a decade. He is a closed book.

"I was not aware of his wish to return to Germany, or his original homeland, or wherever it is he wants to go. I confess that intrigues me. Allie is right when she assumes that I wouldn't mind going along. You see, I still am curious. I would have bet my life that I could have changed that man a little by marrying him. But that sweet, shy disposition that so drew me to him from the beginning turned to a fierce protectiveness, a privacy, a wall around his, his—the—his being itself, if you will. I'm telling you, the man is locked up tighter than a drum.

"I know what Mr. Hampshire, is it—?"

"Haymeyer," Allyson corrected.

"Haymeyer is driving at, warning Allie to be careful. I know none of us wants to admit our fear, but we have to. If we're going to let Allyson pursue this, or you for that matter, Philip, you are going to have to know who and what you are dealing with. We all fear that he might have been a Nazi. And the terrifying nights I lived through with him—though I thank the Lord he never laid a hand on me—nearly convince me that he could have been in Hitler's army.

"There's a slight hitch to that, though. Is it possible that a man with a history like that could never slip up once and say something that would give himself away? There is no doubt in my mind that his American name is not the same as the one he brought with him when he emigrated from Germany. He would not even admit that. But I know it's true."

"You *know* this?" I said. "It's more than a logical guess?"

"Yes."

"Forgive me, but how do you know?"

"Well, it started with the black eyes."

"The black eyes?"

"When I first saw Curtis, the time Allie told you about, at the factory, he still had traces of black and blue rings under his eyes. I could hardly see them in the dim light on the cutting line, but when I hugged him, I got a better look. The first time we went out was at night, and I didn't get to confirm it. But about a week later on a picnic, I noticed that it was almost gone. But there is no doubt both eyes had been blackened."

"Mother, you never told me this."

"It didn't seem significant, honey."

"I don't see how it ties in," I said. "I'm sorry."

"Well, I couldn't even get Curtis to admit that he had been injured. He denied that the traces of bluish and yellow marks around his eyes were even there. He told me it was my imagination, but when I tried to touch them lightly to show him where I meant, he pulled away. I let it drop, but I went behind his back to others in the factory to see what they knew."

"You asked his *friends* about him?" Allyson said.

"People you didn't even know?"

"Well, he didn't have any real friends," Mrs. Scheel said. "And hardly any of them would talk to me. They thought I had come on too strong with him and that I was brassy to be talking to them about him behind his back.

"The personnel manager said no one had ever seen Curtis mad, ever raise his voice, or even seem upset, and he'd been on the job maybe four or five months by now. He took everything in stride, almost too much so. Some of the guys thought they could never count on him if they wanted to file a grievance or something."

"How did he explain it?" I asked, looking at Allyson, who appeared completely nonplussed.

"Just like every other puzzle in his life," her mother said. "He didn't. He ignored the questions, brushed them off, or just made up an obvious tale to let you know you had asked him something he would never answer. I never met a more stubborn, self-contained person in my life. I might have been able to live with it if he hadn't been so full of pain and remorse, but when you combine that kind of guilt with a closed personality, you have one sick person. I couldn't handle it. I wish to this day I could have had more strength, but I exhausted every trick I knew."

"They weren't tricks, Mother. You used your personality, and you were loving him."

"You're right about that," Mrs. Scheel said, looking away and growing quiet. "He just frustrated me so," she whispered. "Maybe that irks me more than anything. He was such a challenge. I loved to make him laugh, even just to smile. He never got any attention from anyone else. There wasn't a person alive I couldn't draw out, and sometimes I think I finally left just because he defeated me, but then I realize that he didn't do it intentionally. There is something stopping the man from opening himself to anyone, even a woman who loved him with everything she had in her—"

Mrs. Scheel's voice broke, and she hid her face in her hands. She was not crying, really, but she had to compose herself before she could speak again. Allyson knelt by her and put an arm around her.

"Why do you assume he changed his name?" I asked. "You knew his first name was Americanized in its spelling, but what about the last name?"

"Well, the only other thing the personnel man told me about Curtis was that it took a long time to get his application cleared through social security and the immigration service because of his name change. Of course, he could not—and would not—divulge Curtis's original name. Once Curtis got his papers and his social security card and was naturalized, that too was a closed book. He seemed more relieved than proud, and if he had been evasive about his German name before, now he was stony. The most I ever got out of him was that his German name had probably either been made up or assigned to him at the orphanage. I don't believe he even really thinks that, otherwise, how does he think he's going to trace his heritage?"

"Do we know that's what he wants to do?" I said.

Neither woman said anything.

Allyson moved back to the love seat. "Philip," she said, "I have withheld from Mother two things."

"What?" Mrs. Scheel demanded.

"Please, Mother, you promised. I want to know if Philip thinks I should tell you."

"Oh, hey," I said, "that's out of my league. I don't know what you've kept from her, and I'm not sure I want to know, but I would guess she has withheld an item or two from you as well."

The women looked at each other. Beatrice lowered her eyes. Then she smiled slightly. "Are we about to work a deal?" she asked.

"I think we'd better," Allyson said. "Just from the new things I've heard tonight I feel more determined to get to the bottom of this."

"How do you feel about the possibility that we all might suffer from what we find?" Mrs. Scheel said.

"I agree that's paramount," I said.

"We couldn't suffer more, could we?" Allyson said. "Mother, you have pain and emptiness from a one-sided relationship. Father is going to explode before he dies if he doesn't drag his poisonous memories into the light of day. And I'm loving and pitying a man I never got to know. He's a father who wasn't a father, a man with no history, no future, no goals. A man who left me without half a family. Maybe it's selfish, Mother, but I have to know. If we can find out without hurting him, and I know there's no guarantee, I think I want to pursue it."

Mrs. Scheel stared at me and then at Allyson. She sipped her cold tea and touched cup back to saucer with a cultured tick. She took it back to the kitchen and returned. My eyes met Allyson's, and it was obvious we were both hoping for the same thing—her mother's agreement that something had to give.

"I'll go this far," her mother said, one knee resting on the arm of the love seat. "I'll tell you the only other significant memory I have of your father if you tell me what you haven't told me yet."

Chapter Thirteen

Allyson told her mother the story of the shoeboxes. Mrs. Scheel nodded sadly throughout. "I know that shoebox," she said finally. "I saw it a few times myself. Once I even caught him clipping items from the paper to put into it. So we shared the same secret, Allie."

They clasped hands, comforting each other.

"I don't mind telling you I'm still in the dark," I said, "but I don't want to press."

"I'm sure Allyson came to the same conclusion I did when she saw the material. It was the only part about Curtis that didn't fit. He was so secretive about everything else, yet that shoebox full of newspaper clippings and old photographs from Germany was so loosely hidden under the bed that it was as if he were begging for it to be found.

"I asked him once if he wanted to talk about it, and it sent him into one of his silent, softly crying hours. 'No,' he said eventually, 'I just feel drawn to my homeland. I keep articles about it here. The pictures are of people they tell me were my family. But there is no resemblance. I do not believe them. But they are pictures of Germans, and so I keep them.'

"But he did more than keep them. Every few months I would see him with the box, studying the photographs. Once when he was gone I dug out the box and studied the pictures. I disagreed with him. I saw a family resemblance, and I think I even saw Curt as a young boy. The face was different, but I was convinced it was him. The names of the people in the pictures had been scratched over and marked out, and there had even been some erasing. I couldn't make out any names, only dates. Mostly the pictures were taken in the early nineteen thirties. The unmarked ones could have been later."

"What kinds of clippings did he save?" I asked.

Allyson and her mother looked at each other and then at me. They started to speak together, but the older woman deferred. "I have photocopies in my folder," Allyson said. She went to get it.

I didn't know what to say to her mother while Allyson was gone. It didn't seem right to talk about Mr. Scheel, so I talked about the only other thing that had been on my mind the last two days. "You have a very beautiful daughter."

Mrs. Scheel smiled. "I know," she said, not immodestly. "And let me tell you something from an admittedly biased point of view, Mr. Spence. I raised that girl, I trained her in the business, I have been her boss, and now we are partners. We have lived together, we have lived apart, and I have given her her freedom. Still no one knows her like I do. That beauty is deep inside her, too. It goes right to the soul."

I wanted to tell her that I sensed it, that I didn't doubt her in the least, but Allyson returned. She could tell by the quick silence that we had been talking about her, but she was so intent on the file folder that she ignored it.

Though only a half-inch thick, the folder had that heavy feel of a sheaf of photocopies. She and her mother sat together and waited as I leafed through it. The photos had been ganged about five to a page. They showed working-class Germans in typical group-shot family poses, very slight smiles when smiling at all. The progression seemed to show a small family of perhaps five, the children growing larger and the parents a little older in each of about a dozen shots. The photocopy of what had been written on the backs of the pictures was nearly useless. Tiny year listings from the 1930s were all I could make out.

The newspaper clippings were the shockers. They weren't the scrapbook style clips an immigrant would save, fun little features and picture-story travelogues of his homeland. No, these were follow-up stories on World War II in Germany. They chronicled the rise and fall of the Third Reich. They were clippings of not just big, front page articles about Hitler and the SS, but also little three-inch items from the back pages of the old *Chicago Sun* and the *American,* the *Daily Tribune* and the *Daily News*. Many were dated before Curtis Scheel had claimed to even have arrived in the United States, so he had obviously obtained back copies. But the clips were also as recent as the late sixties when Allyson had found the box.

"I'd love to see what's in there today," Mrs. Scheel said. "If Allyson retained your firm, could we find out?"

"Probably not," I admitted, not looking up from the photocopies. I shuddered at the abundance of short pieces about the discovery of Nazis in the US and Canada and other countries, their trials, their convictions and acquittals. Mr. Scheel had a file of clips on the Adolf Eichmann trial that would have rivaled that of any library, yet the clips had been neatly folded in a shoebox under a bed for more than a decade when Allyson had found them.

I spent a depressing half hour trying to speed read the file. "I don't think I'm going to be able to show this to Earl," I said, "even if you let me take it. He will not use evidence gained illegally, and under the circumstances, this could be very damaging. I don't know what other conclusion to draw from this, and I frankly don't know, Allyson, what good you'll be doing yourself or your mother or your father to have us confirm this. The man seems to have a very valid reason for living in fear. Maybe the orphanage story is a sham, if these photos of what look like his family are any indication. But if he has been able to maintain silence all these years, even from the woman he was married to, I don't think we'll do him any service by trying to purge his tormented mind with a confession. He has had every opportunity to come forward."

"Do you have to expose him based on what you know?" Allyson asked.

"Earl doesn't think so," I said. "And I feel no

compulsion to, though there would be many who would disagree and would want to see him brought to trial. I suppose if there were evidence that he wasn't remorseful and was just gleefully living off the fat of the land and flaunting his freedom, I would feel differently. Frankly, I think the man is in his own prison and is suffering as much as any jury could impose upon him."

"But I want him out of that prison," Allyson said.

"You'll just be putting him in a literal one," Mrs. Scheel countered.

"Maybe not," Allyson said. "If we can arrange it that Philip and Mr. Haymeyer can find out who Father really is and can confront him with it, perhaps he can experience some kind of emotional release. We can't testify against him, and I'd much rather have it be we who expose him than someone else."

"What makes you think someone else is onto him?" Mrs. Scheel said.

"Because he lives in such fear and torment."

"Because he may be guilty of heinous crimes. We may be interpreting the guilt as fear. Maybe he is less fearful after having eluded prosecution for more than thirty years."

"Well, if he travels internationally on his phony name, he may run into trouble he hasn't expected," Allyson said.

"In Germany?" her mother asked. "And he's had that phony name longer than he had his original. It's official in the US. He's been naturalized with it, he has papers, official ones, with that name all over them. It *is* his name now."

"You forget, I found he's not going to Germany. It's the one other thing I haven't told you. And it's going to convince you that Father needs protection."

"What *are* you talking about, Allie?" Mrs. Scheel said.

"I'm talking about the fact that I wouldn't worry so much if Father were flying nonstop to Germany, but he's not. It's not even on his itinerary."

"I'll bite," her mother said. "Where's he going that's going to put him in danger of being exposed?"

"Israel," Allyson said. "More specifically, Jerusalem."

Her mother drew a hand to her mouth.

"He is booked on a Zion Air nonstop from New York to Tel Aviv, and he has arranged for a car and a driver to take him immediately to Jerusalem. He's reserved a room for four nights at the King David Hotel, and his return flight has been left open. That's all I know. I don't know what or whom he is going to see, but I know I want him either confronted before he leaves or guarded while he's there. I have no idea how a German could be discovered and exposed after thirty years in the United States, but I have a feeling deep inside me that this is an unwise trip for him. Mother, do you agree that we should put Mr. Haymeyer's agency on this to either talk Father out of it or follow him to Israel?"

Mrs. Scheel couldn't talk. I didn't know what to say.

"Mother, I know what you're thinking," Allyson said. "When it finally hit home what all this was about, and I started considering the possibility that my worst fears were true, my first thought was of all the Jewish women we have dealt with over the years on the North Shore. From customers who are the backbone of our business, to associates, to suppliers, to service women, to seamstresses, can you imagine the impact if they knew the history of our own flesh and blood? And you know I'm not thinking in the least about the business impact."

"Of course I know that, Allie," the older woman said. "I know exactly what you're saying. Sweetheart, this whole thing has been on your initiative from the start. I think you have to do what you have to do. I'll support you either way. All I ask is that you keep me informed and don't ask me for any more information."

"You've given Philip all you have anyway, haven't you?"

"Almost."

"Let me have it all," I said. "Please. Don't make this any more difficult for us than it already will be."

Mrs. Scheel studied her hands. "It may be nothing," she began slowly, "but, Allie, do you recall that your father never wore short-sleeved shirts?"

"I guess so, yes. I never thought much about it because he was almost always dressed up when I saw him."

"If you think about it, you'll know that you *never* saw his bare arms."

"OK—"

"Well, I did, and sometimes I think I am the only person who ever did. Philip, did Hitler's troops have any sort of swastika or other insignias tatooed on their forearms?"

"I really don't know. I'd have to check that. Why? Did he have anything like that?"

"No, but he had one of the nastiest burn scars on his forearm that I have ever seen. It was so clean, in a perfect rectangle, that it almost looked as if it had been done intentionally to cover something. I asked him about it only once. He said he had no memory of it whatever. He assumed it was a birthmark, but if it was, it was unlike any I've ever seen."

Chapter Fourteen

"So, I hope you don't mind that I didn't get to those case files you asked me to read," I concluded the next morning.

"Nah," Earl said. "It looks like you're going to be busy enough for a while. Is Allyson coming up to sign the papers?"

"I assume. You want me to pay her a visit?"

"Maybe. But first let me see that folder with the photocopies of the stuff from the shoebox."

"You're kidding. I told Allyson and her mother that you probably wouldn't want to see it, knowing your feeling about using evidence that was gained illegally."

"What are you talking about, Philip? This is a whole different ballgame from when Allyson first talked to us. We're not trying to find out who or what her father is or has done. That's not our problem. Our assignment is protect the man. Any and all information Allyson or Mrs. Scheel can give us that will help us protect him, we want."

"And if it shows that he is a Nazi?"

"We'll deal with that at that time. Frankly, I don't think—from what you've said about the contents of the

125

box—that anything in there will give him away. It may show that he's a German, and maybe even that he was not really an orphan, but lots of people collect news stories about Germany. I have a little nephew who knows more about Hitler than anyone I know."

Earl studied the file carefully, spending most of his time on the photographs. "I'd really like to know if these were taken in Germany," he said. "It would be helpful to know if the little boy in this picture and the older boy in this one are both Mr. Scheel as a child. If they are, and these were taken in his original homeland—and it's not Germany—maybe he really was an orphan, deserted by his parents or left alone when they died or something."

"How will that help us, Earl?"

"It might help us track him."

"But Mrs. Scheel is sure he changed his name."

"And she's probably right, but why did he change it? Who in his hometown, maybe the oldtimers, would recognize the people in these pictures? If you could find that out first, you might be able to save yourself a trip to Israel."

"But what if I go to Austria or Germany or some-place, and then still have to go to Israel? That could get pretty expensive for Allyson."

"Let's let her be the judge of that. Go see her."

I couldn't think of anything I'd rather do, and was grinning to myself—which isn't easy if you think about it—as I moved quickly out of Earl's office and over to my desk to throw on my suit coat. I walked right past Margo, hardly noticing her. "Good morning," she said, formally.

I realized immediately that I should be acting a little more deliberately and mournfully too, the day after breaking my engagement. I let my shoulders sag. "Hi," I said softly. "How are you?"

"Fine."

"Good. That's good. I want you to be fine."

"I am."

"Good."

"Thank you."

"Right."

"I'm really OK, Philip. Don't worry about me."

"Oh, I wasn't. I mean, well, I *was,* but OK, I won't."

"Fine."

"Good." I felt like a jerk. I *was* a jerk. She raised her eyebrows as if she was finished with this ridiculous conversation if I was. So I put on my suit coat and hurried downstairs, realizing only when I caught a glimpse of my reflection in the plate glass window of the boutique that my coat collar was sticking straight up in the back. I tried to straighten it with one hand and open the door with the other.

Allyson was on her way out. "I was just on my way up to see you," she said, reaching for my collar and helping smooth it down. I had never been so close to her. I smelled her delicate perfume and was inches from her eyes. If it hadn't been for the concern evident on her face, I could have savored the moment. "I just got a call from my friend in Evanston—the travel agent—and I have to talk with you and Mr. Haymeyer. Is it all right?"

"Sure," I said, spinning on one heel and leading her

back out the door. I could hardly keep up with her and wound up following her into Earl's office. If Margo looked up, it wasn't until we had passed her.

"Good morning," Earl said.

"Hi," she said quickly, sitting down without taking off her coat. "I need to retain your firm immediately and have my father followed to Israel. I'm afraid for his life."

"Whoa," Earl said. "Easy. Let's take it from the top."

"I got a call from my travel agency friend in Evanston this morning. She said she thought I might want to know that while my father was booked on a flight to Tel Aviv from New York on December fifteen, he was also wait-listed on one this evening. A seat opened, and he's going. She checked with the agency in Chicago that booked him and found that he had already changed all his arrangements, hotel, driver, everything, so he could fly tonight and arrive there tomorrow."

"Allyson," Earl said slowly, trying to change the pace, "none of us is dead certain about your father. We don't know if he's German, though it's obvious he grew up there from his accent alone; we don't know he was an orphan, though we have no solid reason to doubt him; we don't know he was a Nazi, though he could have been in Germany during Hitler's reign of terror, and he would have been the right age for military service."

"And he is a tormented man with a haunting past," Allyson said.

"All right," Earl said, "but are you certain his life

will be in danger if he visits Israel? My point is, are you sure you want to invest in air fare, meals, lodging, and miscellaneous expenses, plus, let me see, two hundred and ninety plus half of that again, carry the one, four hundred and thirty-five dollars a day to have him tailed?"

Allyson dug a pocket calculator out of her handbag. "If it took three weeks, that would be a little over nine thousand dollars, plus expenses. I think I can afford to have one of you go there and stay as long as he can afford to stay."

"And that's what you want to do? Send one of us to protect him?"

"Without his knowing it," Allyson added.

"That may not be easy after a while," Earl said. "Especially if we need to keep a close watch on him. And you know, we guarantee nothing, especially with only one of us going. There's no way one man can watch another twenty-four hours a day unless they're handcuffed together and sleep at the same time."

"I understand, but I'll expect you to do your best."

"I'm not going to be able to go," Earl said. "I'll be sending Philip."

Allyson turned and looked me full in the face, unsmiling. "That makes me feel very secure," she said.

I couldn't pull my eyes away. I wanted to tell her without saying a word that I would do everything in my power to protect her father, as if I were protecting her.

"You can't take your gun, Philip," Earl was saying. I reluctantly turned to look at him. "There's no way they'll let you on a plane to Israel with a firearm, and they'll check your bags too, so forget it. You're going to be on your own over there."

"How am I going to get there if seats are so tight on the airlines?"

"I asked my friend to put you as high on the wait list as she could without getting in trouble," Allyson said. "She's gonna call me later this morning. In fact, maybe I'll call her now." She stood.

"Would you sign this, please?" Earl said, turning a clipboard toward her. She leaned over the desk and wrote her name in a small, neat script.

"How much do you need in advance?" she asked.

"Figure fifteen hundred for air fare, including Chicago to New York, and another six or seven hundred for hotel and meals and transportation for a few days. My hope is that if Philip learns anything in Israel about your father, perhaps he can talk him into coming back soon. That will be cheaper."

Allyson looked dubious about that as she quickly wrote out a check to the EH Detective Agency for thirty-two hundred dollars. "I'll let you know as soon as I hear about the Air Zion flight," she said. "It leaves New York at eight tonight, so you'd better get an early afternoon flight out of O'Hare."

Bonnie booked me on a New York flight for one o'clock while I was packing. "Take enough for four days so you can travel light," Earl had said, "then get to know the valet in the hotel. You'd better stay at the King David and plan to spend a lot of time in the lobby so you'll know when Scheel's leaving."

I was ready to go by ten o'clock and sat fidgeting at my desk. "Have a nice trip, and be careful," Margo said.

"Thanks," I said. "Hey, I hardly noticed how young you look. You startin' high school today?"

"Yeah. I'm nervous. Scared is a better word for it."

"Me too. We've finally hit the big time, huh?"

"Well, I wouldn't put working undercover as a high school girl in the same league with globetrotting after war criminals, but, yeah, I'd say we're at least full-fledged junior deputies by now."

We smiled at each other, and I wondered if mine looked as pained as hers. I hoped it was just a result of anxiety over her assignment, but I knew better.

We both spun toward the door as Larry Shipman bounded up the stairs and blasted through in his characteristic style. "Bonnie, my love, how are ya?" he shouted, winging past her without looking, trenchcoat tails trailing him. "Philip, Margo," he said in greeting as he blew past and into Earl's office. He shut the door.

"He didn't look at me," Bonnie said. "He always looks at me when he comes in. That must mean bad news."

"Oh, don't be ridiculous," Margo said, stealing a knowing glance at me. "It could just as easily be good news, or, knowing Ship, no news." Bonnie turned back to her typing, obviously unconvinced.

Earl stuck his head out. "Bon," he called, "did the morning paper ever come?"

I started to remind him that he had picked it up on the way in when we both arrived at about seven, but he stared me to silence.

"I don't see it anywhere," she said. "Anyone else seen it?"

Margo shook her head.

I didn't know what Earl was up to, so I stalled. "Today's paper, you mean?" I said.

"Bonnie, would you run and get me one?" he said. "And while you're out, could you run my car over to the Standard station? Tell him I want that lube job special they're advertising. They'll bring you back."

"Sure," Bonnie said, "and then will you tell me what Larry has found?"

"You'll be among the first to know," Earl said.

As soon as Bonnie was out the door, Earl motioned Margo and me into his office with a nod. "Tell 'em, Ship," he said as we sat down.

"Bad news," Larry said. "It was as I suspected. Greg had been gone not ten minutes—and the daughter, Erin, about five—when loverboy Bizell shows up in the 'Vette. He was in there for an hour or so, and I was getting impatient. I put a ring of keys on my belt and put on an old cap. I was already wearing grubbies. I picked the lock with Earl's famous steel piece that's quicker and quieter than a key, and as I swung the door open, I hollered, "Maintenance! Anybody home?"

Chapter Fifteen

Margo and I sat there with our mouths open. Was there no end to Shipman's imagination, let alone his gall?

"So they'd been sitting on the couch. She jumps up off his lap, and he stands up, too. 'What *is* it?' she demands, 'and what do you mean, barging in here without knocking?' Bizell looks like he's seen a ghost.

" 'I'm so sorry, ma'am,' I said. 'Just checkin' to see if you got any water from the leak upstairs.'

" 'No,' she says, 'I didn't even know about it.'

" 'That's all I needed to know,' I said, and there was a lot of truth to that. 'Sorry to bother you, Mr. and Mrs.— uh—ah—' and I'm checking a slip of paper. Bizell says, 'Gibbons,' so I repeat it, backing out into the hall. Then I came here."

Margo was angry. "That woman," she said. "Casting aspersions on her husband's reputation when it's been her all along!"

"We can't be certain Greg is totally innocent," Earl said. "But I'm afraid you're right. How would you like to have to tell Bonnie this?"

"You wouldn't do that to me, would you, Earl?"

133

"Of course not. I run the place. I authorized the free service. I relay the bad news. The thing that never ceases to amaze me is the number of times you turn up things in a case that are the opposite of what you thought you were after."

We sat in silence. The phone rang at the switchboard outside. Margo, nearest the door, jumped up to get it.

"Philip, it's for you. Allyson from downstairs."

I shouldn't have appeared so eager to talk to her, grabbing the phone from Margo with hardly an acknowledgment. Allyson had bad news, too. This had not been our day. "My friend has us, I mean you, at the top of the wait list," she reported, "but Air Zion is not expecting any no-shows. I guess these are booked so far in advance that people hang onto their reservations."

"Let me punch Earl onto this line," I said. I told him the story.

"Those are seven forty-sevens, aren't they?" he asked. "Surely someone will be sick or late or something. We're talking about a lot of people. More than three or four hundred, right?"

"Yeah," Allyson said, "but we can't bank on that. What if Philip gets to New York and then can't get on? He just has to be on the same plane with Father." She sounded frantic.

"Can you come up here, Allyson?" Earl asked.

"Sure."

We met in his office again.

"There's one more option," Earl said.

"You're not talking about a charter flight, are you?" Allyson said.

134

"Hardly. Even you couldn't afford that. This plan will cost you, though."

"I'm listening."

"You can buy someone's spot on the plane."

"How do I do that? What if Philip tries to talk someone out of his reservation for some money and no one takes him up on it?"

"He couldn't do it that way, anyway," Earl said, "from what I know about Israeli security. He would have to have a ticket in his own name and then prove it with his identification documents. By the way, Philip, you're going over there as a tourist, you know."

"What do you mean?"

"I mean that when they ask you the purpose for your trip, if you say you're playing clandestine bodyguard to a Nazi war criminal, you're not going to get far."

I nodded. "I've never been there," I said. "So, I *will* be a tourist."

Allyson was getting impatient. "I'm sorry, gentlemen, but how are we going to get Philip on that plane?"

"It'll have to come through the travel agency," Earl said. "Your friend is going to have to get on the blower and start calling booked passengers, informing them that a party is willing to pay a certain amount for their reservation. If she can find anyone, the ticket will be rebooked in Philip's name, and he's set."

"She's going to have to get moving on it," Allyson said. "What would be a good offer? I'm willing to pay for it."

"Oh, I would think a hundred dollars or so, plus a

135

hotel room for the night in New York. Whoever you talk into it is going to need a seat on the next available flight to Israel, no doubt. I would advise your friend to call people who appear to be traveling alone. Families will not likely want to split up, even for money, and the individual passenger who is not on a tight schedule might opt for the money and a free night in New York."

"Can I call from here?" Allyson asked.

Earl turned his desk phone around to face her.

Her hands shook as she dialed. She hung up before anyone answered. "It's all right," she said. "I'll call from downstairs. I need to tell Mother what's happening anyway." Still unsmiling, she winked at me on her way out. I was going to miss her. She trotted back and leaned to whisper in my ear. "If I get you on the flight, can I also drive you to the airport?"

"Sure," I said. "O'Hare or JFK?" It almost drew a smile.

I was getting antsy. Within half an hour I would need to be leaving for the airport. There was no sense going to New York unless I was booked to Tel Aviv. I tried reading a file and making some notes, but I was anxious to hear from Allyson. Bonnie was in Earl's office for a long time.

When she came out, she was in tears, red-faced, seemingly in shock. "I can hardly believe it," she said as Margo embraced her. "I'm so ashamed."

"It's not your fault," Margo said, leading her to the coat rack and helping her on with her coat. "She's a grown woman, married fifteen years."

"But she's not going to make sixteen, is she?" Bonnie said, covering her face with her hands.

"Stranger things have happened," Margo said. "Sometimes people are able to forgive and to rebuild." I had always been impressed with Margo's gentleness and spirit of encouragement.

"Earl said I could take the rest of the day off," Bonnie said. "I'm going home."

"Do you need any company?"

"No, thanks. Larry's not going to like sitting at the switchboard with you off at your high school assignment and Philip flying to New York."

"Don't worry about him," Margo said. "It'll be good for him. Let me walk you to your car. I'm going to the school now, anyway. Are you sure you'll be all right?"

Bonnie nodded.

For a few minutes I enjoyed watching Larry try to familiarize himself with the switchboard. He had manned it during the lunch hour before, but it had been programmed to ring on just one line. Now he would have to answer the appropriate phone, transfer calls to Earl, and everything.

I realized I hadn't said good-bye to either woman. I could be gone by the time either returned to work. And when I saw Allyson's slight smile as she appeared at the top of the stairs, I knew I *would* be. I stood as she entered.

"It worked," she said. "My friend found a man who didn't really need to be in Israel until early next week. It's going to cost about two hundred dollars, but it's worth it. I feel a lot better."

"You look a lot better," I said.

"Thanks."

"If that's possible." It was my first even close to bold statement to her.

"Thanks again," she said, smiling. "Ready?"

Earl had been listening from his doorway. "Keep in touch, Philip," he said. "Don't be afraid to call with questions. Our client will pay for it, and she's loaded. Just remember the time change."

I assured Allyson that she could just drop me off in front of the American departure terminal, but she insisted on parking in the garage and walking me to the gate. She was nervous, talking more than usual and continually checking her watch.

"We're OK," I told her. "We're a little ahead of schedule." I suddenly felt very close to her. Probably it was just that our energy and concentration was centered on her father. "I hope I can protect him and that whatever he wants from Israel, he'll get," I said.

She said nothing.

"I'm going to miss you," I said.

She had been staring out at the planes lined up on the runway. "Ah, no, you won't," she said.

"I will," I said, growing bolder. "I'll miss you very much. I'll be eager to get back to see you."

She looked flattered, but only smiled. I had planned to be among the last on the plane, since I had a seat and a reason to linger, but when the boarding call was announced, Allyson looked at her watch, thanked me for "being so sweet," reminded me that my Air Zion ticket would be at the will call desk in New York, shook my hand, and hurried off more quickly than she had moved all day. I hoped maybe she was hiding an emotion she didn't want to admit, but I wouldn't have bet on it.

I tried to sleep on the way to New York, knowing that the long flight to Tel Aviv would take its toll, but it was impossible. By the time I had had my Coke and a snack and an early dinner, we were "beginning our descent," as they say.

I got to the international terminal a couple of hours early, and the sights there were an experience in themselves. It appeared that 90 percent of the passengers were carrying more bags than would be allowed, most were from Israel, and many were religious Jews, dressed in full garb. The place was jammed, as if the plane was about to take off.

Hardly anyone but the desk clerks spoke English, and tired children wailed the whole time. I pulled two photographs of Curtis Scheel from my wallet and began surreptitiously scouting him out.

Forty minutes later, when I finally reached the head of my line, I had still not spotted him. As the girl checked my reservation, I asked if Mr. Scheel had checked in yet.

"I'll check." She entered his name on her video screen. "Two Scheels have checked in and another has a reservation. First initial?"

"C.," I said.

"There are two. Is he from Cleveland?"

"Chicago."

"Yes, Mr. C. Scheel of Chicago has checked in.

139

Would you like to be seated near him?"

"Not necessarily. I was just curious if—"

"I'm sorry," she said. "I couldn't get you near him anyway. That section is filled, and so is the one behind it. I'm afraid you will be forty or so rows behind him."

"That's all right," I said. "That's fine."

I just hoped I would get a look at him before we hit the ground. "What seat is he in?" I asked.

"Seventeen G. Just ahead of the forecabin lavatories."

At security, I was asked the purpose of my trip, whether I had been to Israel before, who had had access to my bags, had anyone given me any gifts, packages, or messages for anyone in Israel, how long was I staying, and on and on. When I was finally cleared and my bag had been checked, I felt relieved. I sat and waited more than an hour and a half to board, and by the time the announcement came, I was already exhausted. I had not seen Curtis Scheel. And it had already been a long day.

He would enter the plane from the front entrance, I from the rear. I knew I would have to mosey up the aisle at some point during the flight and get a look at him. And from that point on, I couldn't let him out of my sight except when he was in his hotel room. He would be vulnerable even there, but I was only one man. I would have to take some chances.

People all around me were reading prayer books and praying quietly. I dug my Bible from my carry-on bag and read, wishing that I was in Israel for pleasure rather than business. So many friends had told me how the

Bible had come alive when they had visited Jerusalem and all the other historic Christian sights. Maybe one day Margo and I would come back to see it as pilgrims.

Margo. Was she still that entrenched in my mind? What was I saying? It's hard to shake the thoughts of a future life with someone, even when that possibility has ended.

The flight was grueling. It was nonstop to Tel Aviv, and there were several meals and various other boredom interrupters, but not enough. I slept for a while, but a feeling of claustrophobia crept up on me, and even after walking around a little, squeezing past other bored passengers in the aisles, I was unable to sleep anymore. Jet lag was hitting me already, and the only thing I had to look forward to over the next several hours was more of the same. I was just getting ready to make my way up to the front section when the lights were turned off, the window shades pulled, and the movie begun.

I thought I would try again when the movie was over, but the plane was kept dark for those who wanted to sleep. Had I blown it already? What if I couldn't get a look at Scheel before going through customs at Ben Gurion Airport? What if the plane was emptied from front to back? He might have twenty minutes on me and get to the King David Hotel first. If anyone knew he was coming and meant him any harm, I could lose him before I ever saw him. I didn't even know whether he was on the plane.

Chapter Sixteen

My muscles ached and my mind was numb as the plane droned on, if a jet can drone at 600 miles per hour. It seemed as if we would never arrive. When the window shades were finally opened and the Middle Eastern sun invaded the cabin, I jumped up to head for the lavatories and to see if I could catch a glimpse of Curtis Scheel. At least, I had to know what he was wearing in case I lost him temporarily in the crowd.

Everyone else had been waiting for daybreak to go to the bathrooms too, so I stood in long lines for more than a half hour. Finally I made it up to the forward cabin. He was not in his seat, but a vinyl flight bag was tucked beneath it. As I snaked back to my seat, a man squeezed past who could have been Scheel, but I didn't want to look too closely for fear he would remember me if he saw me again in Israel.

When we finally touched down, a common expression clouded the faces of the hundreds of passengers. The women's makeup was no longer doing its job. Most of the men needed shaves and wore blank expressions of fatigue that would be remedied only by an afternoon and all-night sleep. I wanted to get to where I would be able to see Scheel as he got off the plane, but sure enough, they let us off from front to back, and he had a big lead on me. Several buses carried us from the runway to the terminal, and he was at least two buses ahead of me.

I hoped the bottleneck at the passport check-in stations might give me a chance to catch him, but I received such hateful stares from the other tired passengers when I tried to get ahead of them that I waited until I got to the baggage claim area to make my play. Though I was among the last to crowd around the two conveyor belts of baggage, no luggage had appeared yet. Even when they did start their mechanized parade, I ignored the bags and scanned the faces. Several times I thought I saw the little man, hidden behind taller people, but I lost him. I moved away from the claim area to the final check-through to ground transportation. If he had been on the plane, he would have to come through here.

And then I saw him, a short, middle-aged man. He wore a dark brown suit with cuffs on the pants, plain black oxford shoes, and a hat. His tie, unlike those of most of the rest of the passengers, was still snug at the neck. He wore an olive sweater vest under his suit coat. The vinyl bag I had seen on the plane was slung over one shoulder, and a modest suitcase was the only other item he carried. It was bound by thin string, almost like a Christmas present. When he passed I turned to watch him from behind. He walked slowly, hesitatingly following others who had found their bags. While he was in line to have his luggage checked at security, I dove into the crowd to find my suitcase, looking over my

144

shoulder every few moments to check on his progress. For a long time he was stalled in the line, but then he seemed to be moving up farther every time I looked.

Finally, he was gone. I had found my bag, but I didn't have time for anyone to pick through it for contraband. I set it and my carry-on piece off to one side and dashed to the inspection area. "Bags?" the guard said.

"No."

He checked my passport quickly, and I ran out into the waiting area for ground transportation. My man was approaching a cab driver. I walked to within earshot when he said, "Can you take me to the King David Hotel in Jerusalem?"

"Many shekels," the driver explained.

"OK," Curtis Scheel said.

I ran back inside and got my luggage, sweated through a careful inspection, and hurried back out. The cabs were filling. A limousine with draped windows idled at the curb. "Is this car for hire?" I asked.

"More than cabs," the driver said. "Happy to take you."

"How much?" I asked.

"How much you want to pay, Mister?"

I didn't have time to bargain. I got in and told him I would pay him extra if he could get close enough to follow a certain cab, even though I hadn't yet figured out the money system. We didn't catch the cab, and I probably got rooked on the fare, but I had no choice.

I asked the registration clerk at the King David if John Scheel had checked in yet.

"No, sir. The only Scheel we have checked in today was a Curtis, who was just put in three eighteen. Would you like to call him or leave a message?"

"No, thank you."

I waited until the head clerk was busy so he wouldn't think I knew Curtis Scheel and make the mistake of saying something to him about my looking for him. I stepped to the counter and was waited on by a young assistant. "Any chance of getting a room on the third floor?" I asked.

"Certainly. Several rooms are available on three. Any preference?"

"What do you have?"

"I'll check. All of the odd teens are open, also the evens except for three sixteen and three eighteen."

"Oh, I don't care. Put me in three seventeen."

"That's a double room, sir. Are there two of you?"

"No. But that's OK. I'll take it."

"Room three eleven is a single for much less money, sir."

"No, that's OK. I'll take three seventeen."

Once settled, I put my ear to the service door connecting my room with Scheel's. He was just climbing into bed, if I could trust my ears. I listened for more than five minutes until he was snoring softly.

I dialed the phone.

"Front desk."

"Double-checking on Mr. Scheel's wakeup call in three eighteen," I said.

"We have no wake-up call recorded for you, sir. When would you like to be called?"

"Oh, no. I'll call you later."

"Very well, sir."

I dragged one half of one of the sectioned double beds over to the service door, then unpacked my suitcase. I hardly had the strength to undress, but when I finally stretched out on the cool sheets, I was asleep within minutes. I hoped my head was close enough to the door that I would be awakened by any noise coming from Scheel's room.

At about 11:00 P.M., I awoke with a start. The room was pitch black, and I had not heard anything. At least I thought I hadn't. Then why had I awakened? I wasn't sure. I sat up and leaned over so my ear was flush with the door to Scheel's room. Sure enough, the bed squeaked as he moved. Was he going somewhere, or was he simply moving in his sleep? I listened without breathing. He dialed the phone.

"Hello," he said. "Can I get food in my room? . . . Call vat? . . . Room service? . . . Vat's de number? . . . T'ank you."

He dialed again. "Vant food in my room," he said. "T'ree hundred and eighteen . . . Vatchu got? . . . Menu? No, I see no menu . . . Just tell me vat you got . . . OK, just tell me sandwiches. I can get sandwich and coffee? . . . OK, OK. T'ank you."

He left the bed, and I heard water running in his bathroom. I took my phone into the closet and dialed room service. "Did you just take an order for room three eighteen? . . . Well, listen, when he delivers, could

147

you have the boy explain the wakeup call system here?"

"I could tell you, sir," the man said.

"No, just have the boy tell when he delivers, OK?" And I hung up.

A few minutes later, ear pressed against the service door again, I heard the puzzled bellman ask Scheel if he had asked about the wakeup call system.

"No. Vat that is?"

"Well, if you want to be awakened at a certain time, you just call the desk downstairs and ask them to call you at that time in the morning."

"I could call them even now?"

"Sure."

"No charge?"

"No charge."

"I to tip you for bringing food?"

"That would be fine, sir."

"How much?"

Scheel obviously held out his hand with change and bills in it. "One of these and one of these will be just right, sir," the bellman said. "You ask around and see if I took too much, OK?"

I wanted to get back to sleep, but I waited until Scheel finished eating to see if he would phone for a wakeup call. "Car and driver to pick me up here at nine in morning," he told the desk. "Can you vake me up vit' phone at eight? . . . T'ank you."

I pulled my bed back to its normal position, called in a 7:30 wakeup call for myself, and slept soundly. When the phone rang, I assumed it was my wakeup call, but my watch said it was only 6:00.

148

"Hello? Seven-thirty already?"

"No, but I couldn't sleep anymore. I've been sleeping since we got here, and now I'm ready for the day to begin."

I sat up and swung my feet off the side of the bed to the floor. "Allyson? Is this you!?"

"Of course."

"Where are you? You sound close!"

"At the Diplomat Hotel."

"In New York? Where?"

"Right here, silly. I'm about five minutes south of you, according to the cab driver."

I was finally awake. "Allyson, you'd better be kidding."

"I'm not."

"What're you doing here?"

"I came to help you. You can't keep an eye on my father yourself."

"But you can't help! If he sees you, it's ruined."

"Philip, I was on your flight to Tel Aviv. I caught a United flight out of O'Hare about fifteen minutes after you took off, and I had my friend pay *two* people to stay off the Air Zion seven forty-seven. If you didn't recognize me, why should my father?"

"I don't believe you."

"I was only a few rows behind you, Philip. I was the little old lady in the burgundy shawl."

"If you were disguised as a little old lady, how did you get past the passport people?"

"I just straightened up and took the scarf away from

149

my face. They probably thought I was one weird young lady to be dressed so frumpy."

"Allyson, I'm having a hard time taking this all in. How come I didn't even see a little old lady in a burgundy shawl?"

"I'll bet you can't describe ten of the people you saw on that plane. You were tired, and nervous, and you were looking for a little man in his late fifties, not a little old lady. And you were concentrating on the front of the plane, not the back."

"I still don't get it, Allyson. If you planned to come with me, why didn't you just tell me?"

"I had to hide from Father anyway, and I was sure you and Earl would not let me."

"We couldn't have stopped you."

"No, but you would have tried awfully hard to talk me out of it."

"True, and I'm going to have to try hard to talk you out of getting too close to your father, too. I don't know if anyone else is following him, or what they might do to him if they are. That's what I'm here for, remember?"

"Philip, I want to see you."

"I want to see you too, Allyson, but I can't have distractions."

"I'm a distraction?"

"You bet your life."

"You wouldn't make me hole up in the Diplomat Hotel when we're this close together and thousands of miles from home, would you?"

"I hope you don't think we're going to get to sightsee or shop or go out for dinner."

"Of course I know we can't do that. I just want to help you, and I want to be kept up to the minute on what's going on with my father. Is that too much to ask?"

"I still can't believe this isn't a dream."

"Did you get enough sleep, Philip?"

"Yeah. Woke up hungry, though."

"Me too. Would you be able to come down here for breakfast, or are you expecting Father to be up and moving soon?"

I told her he was meeting his car and driver at nine and that I would have to be back for that. "I'll be there at seven for breakfast," I said.

I called the desk and double-checked on the wakeup call for 318. It was still for 8:00. I told the clerk to cancel the call for 317.

In the huge lobby of the sprawling Diplomat Hotel, Allyson reached up and grabbed me by the shoulders with both hands. The sun was already fairly high in the sky, and through the lobby windows we could see a man and his camel parked near a tour bus.

"I just saw you off yesterday in Chicago, I know," Allyson said, "but being this far from home calls for a long-lost style greeting, don't you think?"

I wished I had the fortitude to tell her what kind of greeting I really preferred. She looked radiant, though she couldn't hide the concern in her eyes.

Chapter Seventeen

I couldn't get over how pleased I was to see Allyson, even under those circumstances. We enjoyed the typical Israeli breakfast of eggs, cheeses, fruit, and even vegetables.

"How will you keep track of Father today?" she asked.

"One of two ways," I said. "The hard way is to get a cab and tell the driver to 'follow that car.' But with the unrest and tension here, limo drivers are wary of being followed. They don't always know who their passengers are or who might be out to get them, so I might not get far that way. I'm sure a cab driver would try it for the right money, but the limo driver would likely catch on, even if your father didn't notice."

"What are your options?"

"Well, Earl has been training me how to get information about people without lying to get it. I was really having a moral problem with it as a Christian. Earl is one who believes the end justifies the means where the life of someone may depend on what we know and what we do. So he often just tells outright lies. Like last night, he might have tried to duplicate your father's voice on the phone to get information out of the desk clerk. Or he might have told the clerk that your father was his uncle and that he needed to keep an eye on him or that he wanted to surprise him or something."

"Crafty."

"Very. Earl's the best. And in many ways in this business, the end *does* indeed justify the means. But I was raised to tell the truth. So even when I tell a lie for what some may feel is a good cause, I'm not good at it. Of course, I could be trained to get better at it, but it's hard for me to live with."

"So what do you do?"

"I asked Earl to think of an alternative, because I couldn't. It took him a few days, but he came up with one. He tells me to be bold, to ask questions, and let the listener draw whatever conclusions he wants. Like I told the desk clerk I was double-checking on Mr. Scheel's wakeup call. That was entirely true. I had heard your father call it in for eight o'clock, and then I was double-checking it. I didn't say I was Mr. Scheel, and if the clerk wants to think I was, it doesn't bother me. When I asked the room service manager to have the bellman explain the wakeup service, I didn't say Mr. Scheel had requested it. I just told him to do it."

"So, how will that help you this morning? Can you avoid the risk of the 'follow that car' routine?"

"I'm thinking about it."

"Good luck."

"Thanks."

Allyson and I were finished eating, and apparently

finished talking, too. I looked at my watch, and she looked at hers. "I would appreciate your staying close to the hotel here today," I said. "I don't know where your father is going, but it would be very dangerous, or at best unfortunate, for you to run into him if you're out and about."

"Could you call me and tell me where he's gonna be when you know? Then maybe I can get out to a museum or something. I'll go crazy just sitting here waiting."

"I'll see what I can do."

We were silent again. I had about twenty minutes before I had to start heading back to the King David. I looked into Allyson's eyes. There was nothing to say, but the shyness was gone from both of us. I had no idea if she was feeling for me what I was feeling for her, but I was past the point where I was uncomfortable looking at her for longer than a moment. Usually I looked away after a few seconds, and more often, she looked away. Now we simply stared at each other from across the table. I put my hand over hers. She didn't pull away, but she didn't respond, either. I smiled at her, wondering if I had surprised her. When the waiter came, the moment was lost.

We strolled through the lobby again, and Allyson took a picture of the camel through the glass. I wanted to hold her hand, but I didn't want to push her or scare her. I was dying to know what she was thinking, feeling. "I gotta go," I said.

"I'm sorry," she said, softly.

"About what?"

"That you have to go."

"That makes me feel good," I said.

"It was meant to."

"You're very forthright, aren't you?"

"So are you," she said.

"I think you're special," I said.

"I am," she said, burying her head in my arm and giggling. People turned to look. I laughed.

"How long has it been since I've been free to act like a child?" she said.

She was suddenly serious.

"What is it?" I asked.

"You have to go, and I'm battling two emotions. I'm scared and upset and troubled about Father. I keep having second thoughts about your being involved, but as Earl says, your assignment is to protect him, not to expose him. And then here I am acting like a schoolgirl because I like being around you. That's hard to keep straight in my head, one feeling so dark and threatening, and the other so pleasant."

"I'm facing exactly the same problem," I said. "I need to be razor sharp to handle this case, and yet I think about you all the time."

"You do?"

"I wouldn't have, maybe, if you hadn't come to Israel."

"I'm sorry. I had to."

"I'm glad you did."

"Me too," she said. "And like I predicted in your office just a few days ago, I'm getting to like you, Mr. —" she teased.

156

"Spence," I reminded her.

"Right. Mr. Spence. Now get going. And if you can call me and tell me where I can go without running into Father, that'll help."

"I will. 'Bye." She gripped my hand and made me pull away to get in the cab. I wished I didn't have to work.

"You here to pick up Mr. Schwartz?" I asked the first limo driver in line at the King David.

"No, Mr. and Mrs. Young," the driver said.

I asked the second the same question.

"No, sir," he said. "Mr. Scheel."

"You're not with Feinstein Livery?"

"No, sir. I'm with Carmel Touring."

"Thank you."

I jogged into the lobby and called Carmel Touring. While I waited for them to answer, Scheel walked out past me, hesitating and half-stepping and looking around as usual. He asked at the desk if the limo driver would come in or wait for him outside. "He may come in if you're late," the man said. "Otherwise, he'll be outside."

As he went out the door and the limo drivers called to see if he was their man, a woman answered my call. "Carmel Touring."

"Double-checking on Mr. Scheel's itinerary today," I said.

"Is that Mr. and Mrs. S. Scheel, or C. Scheel?" she said.

157

"C."

"Starting the day at the Yad Vashem Memorial. The rest of the day is open, the car available until four-thirty this afternoon."

I took a cab to Yad Vashem, not realizing until I arrived that it consisted of various beautiful memorials to the martyrs of the Holocaust. Inscriptions, sculptures, even planted trees had been placed in this setting to commemorate the six million who had been massacred by the Nazis in World War II for their "crime" of existing as Jews. I confess I was shaken to the core to realize that Curtis Scheel would come here. I had hardly been aware of the museum and the various remembrances, and now I was face to face with them, realizing the limits of my own knowledge of the tragedy. We had studied it in school, sure, but there was something sacred and eerie and soul-twistingly somber about this place. And it hadn't even opened to the public for the day yet. Curtis Scheel joined the crowd of a couple of hundred or so who milled about the Warsaw Ghetto Memorial Square. There were school children, tourists of several nationalities, religious Jews in varying styles of dress, and perhaps some survivors or children of survivors. No doubt, there were also in the crowd some relatives of the martyrs.

Scheel stood away from the rest, gazing somewhat confused—I thought—at a modernistic sculpture on the Wall of Remembrance. I studied it for several minutes, trying to put together what little I knew about Jewish symbolism and art, and the best I could make of it was that it honored the Jews who rebelled against the Nazis in Poland rather than submitting to their barbarism.

When the doors finally opened, many filed slowly into a huge dark room where nonreligious Jews and Gentiles whose heads were uncovered were given cardboard caps. I had trouble keeping mine on, but I soon forgot about it as I stared at the flame and the markers that plotted the concentration and death camps that had dotted all of Europe during the domination of the Third Reich. An English-speaking guide quietly told his group about the various places and the atrocities committed there. It was moving, but I had to keep watching Scheel. He stood rigidly, directly across from the marker for Chelmno. After several minutes he moved down to stand before the marker for Treblinka. I remembered these names, not as famous as Auschwitz or Buchenwald, but names from history lessons nonetheless. I wondered what memories they conjured for Mr. Scheel.

As the crowd moved slowly and silently out, many of us dropping our cardboard caps back into a box, Scheel lagged behind. As his driver and car waited in the parking lot with many others, he sat on a bench outside the museum itself and stared at the ground. Oh, to know what was going on inside that head. Was this his final purging? Did he want to see what the Jews had put together in their museum to force themselves and the world to remember? Would he be moved to any sort of confession in his soul, not the subconscious type that had violated his dreams for years, but the kind that might wring out his being and bring him to his knees before his victims?

A tour group with a German-speaking guide moved into position before the artwork that graces the wall that separates the two wings of the museum. When Scheel heard the explanation of the symbols in the art and the story it told of Jewish persecution through the years, he rose heavily and edged close enough to get the whole presentation. He appeared puzzled, as I must have, even when I heard the English tour guide talk about it. There was something strangely beautiful about the stark sculpture on the wall, and I remembered how meaningless it had appeared before I heard someone point out the elements.

There was something strange, too, about the crowds that moved through the museum. They went in from our right, knowing full well that they were going to get an eye-opening educational experience, but having no idea of the emotional impact it might have on them. They chatted quietly with each other, smiling, though basically reverent. No one was acting inappropriately, but there were incidental conversations. As they came out into the open again from the first leg of the tour and headed into the final portion, those of us waiting to get in saw them afresh. They walked more slowly. They spoke not at all. Some looked on the verge of tears, most appeared stunned. It made me more curious than ever to see what awaited us, and I wondered anew what effect it would have on a Nazi. How many had slipped in unnoticed to see it?

Chapter Eighteen

Just more than a dozen people entered the museum with Curtis Scheel. I stayed behind him and out of his line of vision no matter where he turned. I realized quickly that I should have tried to go through the facility alone first so I wouldn't be tempted to stop and look at the stark, high contrast blowups of black and white photographs and read the captions. This, I realized, made up the bulk of the museum, and I was fascinated.

But I had to keep Scheel in view. I stole glances at some of the first photographs, documenting Nazi oppression of the Jews in Europe before the camps had opened. Signs calling for the blood of the Jews and banners with derogatory slogans against the Jewish race gave evidence that the Nazis quickly quit trying to hide their reasons for wanting to do away with the Jew. They didn't trump up charges against him. They didn't frame him or entrap him. They didn't push him into wrongdoing. They needed no other excuse than that he was a Jew. That was enough. That was punishable by death.

I put myself in a position where I could watch the movement of Scheel out of the corner of my eye as I read and studied the photographs. He was not twenty-five feet into the gallery when his already slow pace simply stopped, and he stood staring at the photographs, laboring to read the English captions. He had no trouble with the German phrases and words in the pictures themselves.

He stood granitelike as other patrons filed past, reading more quickly, taking in the flow and progression of the story. It was education, it was history. It was moving and dramatic, and it assaulted their eyes, taught them lessons, opened their minds. But it did nothing to them compared with what it did to Curtis Scheel.

It became obvious that he could barely take it in. I moved closer to the wall and pretended to be trying to get a better view of a small photograph, but I really wanted a look at his face, at least from the side.

He was simply staring at a picture of a young Jew and his German girlfriend who had been caught together in the man's apartment. They had been forced to wear signs in public, admitting their "disgraceful" relationship. Scheel stared at the picture, and his face grew taut. He squinted, his eyes darting around the background of the shot, perhaps remembering landmarks of his youth. Finally he moved slowly along and stopped at the next picture.

He spent several minutes at each one, seemingly unable to move away until something inside him had assimilated what his eyes had taken in. His entire body was more rigid. He seemed unable to bend his legs at the knee, walking slowly like a robot, sometimes seeming to hardly move. All it did was make me want to study the photographs even more and read the captions more carefully, but I didn't dare linger lest he suddenly regain his composure and slip out with the dozens who had passed him in the last several minutes.

I almost forgot I was there to protect him. From what or whom, I didn't know. I doubted that anyone recognizing him, regardless who Scheel really was or had been, would try to harm him there, but stranger things had happened. I moved closer to him. We had been in that section of the photo gallery, a blackened room with small lights illuminating the photographs, about three times longer than the usual spectator. Scheel arrived at the photos of families who had been forced to dig their own graves, then strip and stand together in line while they were machine-gunned into the holes. I stood transfixed, looking over his shoulder at the pathos evident on the faces of the young mother and father as they tried to comfort terrified children. There could be no explanation, no pacifying. And there was no escape. The parents were stoic, comforting their babies in their arms before the bullets drove them to their deaths.

My throat was tight. I didn't know what I felt toward the Nazis. That emotion that most sane people in the free world nurture deep in their bosom, that outrage and incomprehension of the atrocity, is something that doesn't need explanation. It was simply wrong, dead wrong, unconscionable what the Nazis did to the Jews. And worst of all, there was not even an attempt to justify it. What was I feeling toward Scheel? How could I pity him?

Yet in a sense I did. He had lived with this all of his adult life, and now it was staring him in the face in more vivid and horrible detail than he endured in his worst nightmares. And he wasn't running from it. He couldn't. It had him in its grip, and he was forced to face it. I didn't know if it would be therapeutic or not. All I knew was that it had stopped him in his tracks. Was this the reason he had come to Jerusalem? Had he read about this place, and had he known that it was the link to his past, the only link—painful as it had to be—that would do a number on the demons that tormented him?

As he moved slowly to an even more horrifying picture of hundreds upon hundreds of emaciated bodies in a tangle of arms and legs and torsos, buried stiff in a huge pit, Curtis Scheel drew his right hand slowly to his mouth and completely covered it so his breath was forced through his nostrils. It was as if the hand on his mouth was the only thing keeping his head erect. He nodded in protest, trying to look down or turn away, yet he held his head in place with the fingers that kept his mouth shut. His breath began to come in great draws and blows through his nose, causing some passersby to wonder at him, but he was oblivious to all around him. I stood directly behind him and shielded much of the view others might have had of him. I fought conflicting emotions again of outrage against the Nazis, yet pity for this man who faced the evil in photographs that may have been shot just for him.

His chest heaved, and his loud breath came in broken gusts. When people stared, I stared back, and they moved along. Finally he tore himself from the picture and turned to look at the other side of the room. It was as if he simply couldn't take another closeup view without a break. He had been lingering at horrible depictions for nearly an hour, and his spirit had been stretched to its limits. His eyes were red, the pupils large in the darkness, and he looked me full in the face for the first time, his hand still covering his mouth. I looked away quickly and focused on another photograph.

More people moved past, and finally Scheel turned back to face the display of pictures. When he arrived at a shot of a conveyor belt delivering the cadaver of a naked Jewish man to the door of a crematorium, it was more than he could take. He covered his mouth with both hands now and forced himself to look at the photograph. The man operating the oven held the door open and was shoving the body in with a steel bar. Scheel began to moan, only the hands over his mouth keeping him from being heard throughout the room. The painful cries of mourning came through his nose, and he pushed his hands higher so the noises were pinched off and sounded like the cries of an animal trying to get out of a sealed box.

The more he moaned, the more he tried to stop, but the harder it became. He shut his eyes hard, and his arms tightened to stifle the cries, but it was futile. His head dropped to his chest and great tears gushed from his eyes and cascaded over his knuckles, still pressed against his nose. His whole body shook, his knees bent. People stared and turned away quickly, unable to deal with the

165

anguished cries. The pictures and captions were enough for them. They didn't need this.

I didn't know what to do. I was drawn to embrace him, but I was not ready to give myself away, and I had no idea why I felt such compassion. If he had been responsible for this in any way, he needed this reckoning. It was all he could do to continue breathing while sobbing and trying to stifle his terrible moaning at the same time. He moved back into a tiny alcove where no one would pass him, and I saw him fall to his knees and move his hands up over his eyes. His cries could be heard now by anyone near, so I stepped up to block everyone's view, as if I were his son, protecting his privacy. His fingers trembled and he let the tears fall in giant drops on the floor.

When his sobbing stopped, his tears continued. He worked hard at regaining his composure. He stood, his face still to the wall, and tried to straighten his suit. There would be no hiding the fact that it had been he who had broken down at the sight of this, but when he shuffled back out of the alcove to resume his tour, he sought me out, though I tried to elude him. He leaned close. "Speak English?" he asked.

I nodded.

"I am grateful for your kindness," he said.

I didn't know what to say. How he could be aware during his grief that I had helped in a small way to protect his privacy, I couldn't understand. I touched his shoulder lightly to indicate that he was welcome, and I walked ahead of him. He caught me, ignoring the rest of the photographs in the first half of the museum. "Are you a Jew?" he asked.

I shook my head. If he was looking for someone to talk to, a Jew to apologize to perhaps, I knew he would have little trouble finding one. "This place is run by the Jews," I said, realizing immediately that only an imbecile would not know that. As we moved across the open area to the other side, I pointed to workers and helpers.

He nodded and followed me to another huge room of pictures. "Would you like me to walk with you?" I asked.

"I vould, yes, very much," he said, shyly. I assumed the worst of his emotional trauma was over.

I was wrong.

Chapter Nineteen

Scheel ignored many of the subsequent photographs, but he spent a lot of time laboriously reading the English translations of the captions, particularly under the shots of Nazi leaders. His lips moved slowly as he worked on the quotes of the men trying to defend their murdering of the Jews.

I sensed his body reacting anew, and I wondered if I could shield him again from the stares of others if he broke down. It happened when we encountered first a pathetic shot of a few teenage girls in just their slips, nearly finished disrobing before their executions. Their faces evidenced more confusion than anything, but the fear in their dark eyes reached out to Curtis Scheel's throat and caused him to gasp loudly and turn away.

But he found himself face to face with one of the more grotesque pictures in the collection, a difficult choice in this place where the Jews have chosen to force upon the world in the form of photographs the horror that was forced upon them at the hands of the Nazis while the rest of the planet stood by.

He crossed his arms and hugged his shoulders while he gazed at the image of a woman who had been used by

Nazi physicians as a guinea pig to test procedures and drugs. She was crippled and dying, due only to their callousness. In fact, she was healthier looking than most of the imprisoned women because she had been fed and taken care of to be a better specimen. It was a stark, horrifying thing, and it caused Scheel to run. He pushed past people and charged up the stairs, blindly looking for the exit.

Younger and faster, I zigzagged behind him, staying close. I was the only thing close to a friend he had in this place. He looked wildly from right to left, and when he reached the bottleneck at the exit where people picked up literature and left their contributions, he suddenly slid to a stop and dug deep in his pockets. He still had not changed his American currency into shekels, and he withdrew several large bills, probably totaling more than a hundred dollars. He shoved them into the box, his lips quivering, fighting to keep from sobbing aloud again. He reached for more money.

I gently took hold of his wrist. "This is not the answer," I said. "You will never be able to pay enough."

"I vant to support this shrine," he whined. "The vorld must see this."

"Shalom and thank you very much," a young man at the desk said, reaching across the counter for Scheel's hand.

"Shalom," Scheel said, his voice breaking. "Are you a Jew? Of course you are."

The young man smiled. "Yes, and you?"

I flinched at the irony of that, until I heard Scheel reply.

"Yes, I am a Jew. I am a survivor. I am an escapee." He put both arms on the counter and dropped his head, bursting into tears again.

I was numb.

"Bring him back here," the young man said. His nameplate read Yaacov K. "Call me Jacob," he said. "Are you a relative?"

I was still reeling, lightheaded from this thunderous revelation.

"Yes," Scheel answered for me, and the three of us ducked into an office.

"What camp were you in, sir?"

"You may call me Kurt, vit' a *K*," Scheel said. "The last name is Burghoff, and I vas sent vit' my father and mother and brother and sister to Chelmno, December 8, 1941."

Jacob trotted to a shelf on the other side of the room and pulled down a huge three-ring binder. "Bring the Treblinka book, too," the older man said. "Ve vere transferred there October 4, 1942." Jacob turned back and brought it.

He carefully leafed through the pages of Burghoffs, asking Kurt for the first and middle names of his father and mother and brother. As he reached each name, he paused. "Are you aware of their dispositions, Mr. Burghoff?"

Kurt nodded sadly. "I escaped in the August second revolt vit' a couple of hundret others in 1943, but none of my family reached our meeting point. They vere killed."

My mind raced, frantically striving to put together all that had led all of us to believe the opposite of the truth about this troubled man.

"Here is your confirmation, sir. I'm sorry." Jacob turned the book so Burghoff could read for himself. His father's name and birthplace and date and his death camp number were listed, followed by the notation, "Caught in escape attempt, August 2, 1943, sentenced to death for conspiracy to escape. Executed August 5, 1943."

For his mother, the same, except the execution took place a day later. For his older brother, it read, "Wounded by shooting during escape attempt, August 2, 1943. Executed same day."

"And vere is my name?" Kurt said.

"Right here, sir. It says Kurt Burghoff, born November 12, 1923, Leipzig, Germany, #116075. Reported escaped August 2, 1943. Assumed dead."

Burghoff stood with a swagger, removed his suit coat, and rolled up his sleeve to expose the ugly burn scar his wife had told me about. Jacob looked at it for only an instant and then into the man's watery eyes. Jacob doubled a fist and raised it in the air, a celebration of Kurt Burghoff's defiance.

With the same aplomb, Burghoff rolled the sleeve back down, buttoned it, and replaced his coat.

"I have lived for nearly thirty years vit' the guilt of having escaped vile my family suffered," Kurt said. "How I vish I had been captured again or killed in the escape."

"That's not what your family would have wanted," Jacob said earnestly, his hand on the man's arm. "Let me find your sister's name here, just so your mind will be clear on all of these. Yes, here it is." He turned it and read it as we did.

"Rachael Burghoff, born May 15, 1926, Leipzig, Germany, #116076."

"Ven did she die?" Kurt asked.

Jacob spun the book back around and peered at the listing. "When there is no death date we must check the release book," he said. "I don't want to get your hopes up, Mr. Burghoff, but let me check to make sure. If she is not in the release file, you can assume she was executed or died, and the date was simply not available."

But Burghoff could hardly contain himself. He had lived in guilt and torment for years, and the very idea of a flicker of hope had not entered his mind. Now it crashed down on him with its full force, and he was pulled from his chair once more. He followed Jacob to the release book and hung on his elbow as the young man looked up Rachael's name. As he began to read, Kurt whooped and spun in the air. "She's alive, she's alive!" he shouted.

"Now, take it easy," Jacob said, trying to get more light on the page and read the listing aloud. "Very often we find that people who survived until the Allied victory have since died. Kurt fell silent, and Jacob read: "Rachael V. Burghoff, among the survivors at Buchenwald, where she was transferred after the destruction of Treblinka in late 1943. Married Jonathan Haase, Berlin,

September 23, 1949. Divorced, October 10, 1951. Married Frederich Speigel, Frankfurt, January 16, 1953. Widowed May 24, 1960. Married Michael Nissim, Haifa, Israel, December 20, 1964. Last reported address, 53 Victoria, Haifa, Israel."

Kurt was beside himself. "I must go to see her!" he said. "I must go now!"

"Let us call her," Jacob suggested.

"No! She vill never believe a crazy man on the phone. I must go see her! How far is Haifa? Can I make it today by car?"

"Certainly. But please, Mr. Burghoff, remember that Mrs. Nissim could have moved or even passed away since she last updated her listing. She may be difficult to find."

"No," Burghoff said. "It vould be cruel of God to do that to me now."

He pumped Jacob's hand vigorously and promised to see him again, then he hurried out to the car as I trailed him. "Please let me talk to you before you go to Haifa," I begged.

"Come vit' me," he called over his shoulder.

I debated whether to tell him that his daughter could go too, but I decided against it. As thrilled as she would be to see this reunion, or as much help as she could be if Kurt *was* disappointed, I thought he needed to do this alone. The healing of his immediate family would begin soon enough.

He told the driver to get him to Haifa as fast as possible, then turned to me. "Are you sure you vant to

174

go along?" he said. "I can's guarantee a ride back. I don't know how long I might stay vit' my sister."

I resisted the urge to warn him against wishful thinking and simply told him yes, that I really needed to talk with him. I wasn't sure he could take it with all the emotional upheaval he had already endured and the potentially traumatic meeting with his long lost sister, but I told him straight out that I had been sent to follow him, just for his own safety, by his daughter and with his former wife's approval. I said nothing about their suspicions. He was shocked. And moved.

"Mr. Burghoff," I said, "if you don't mind, I'd like to make a suggestion. I would like to help you locate your sister and then make the first contact with her. It could be very difficult for both you and her if you meet all of a sudden. Just let me prepare her and then bring you in. What do you think about that?"

"I t'ink it will be hard to vait in the car," he said, "but I see the visdom in it, and somehow I trust you, Mr. Spence."

Late that afternoon in Haifa, the driver asked directions to Victoria Street while I dialed the number listed for the Nissims at that address. I prayed the phone book was new and that they still lived there. A young woman, maybe a teenager, answered in Hebrew.

"I'm calling for Mrs. Nissim," I said, slowly, wondering if she could understand English. She did, and called her mother to the phone.

"Hello?"

"Mrs. Nissim, my name is Philip Spence, and I'm

175

here in Haifa from the United States. I have some news for you about an old acquaintance of yours from the States, and I was wondering if I could see you for a few minutes to bring a greeting."

"I have several friends who are now in the States," Mrs. Nissim said. "Can you tell me who the message is from?"

"I'd rather wait until I see you, if you don't mind."

"I guess not," she said, hesitating. "My husband will be here," she added, perhaps as a warning.

"Very well. We'll see you shortly."

My youth and nonthreatening appearance helped put Mrs. Nissim at ease. Her daughter flitted in and out of the room as we talked, and her husband sat reading in the corner. "Mrs. Nissim, I have very good news for you," I began, "probably the best news you've ever had in your life."

She raised her eyebrows. "I have had a very difficult life, Mr. Spence," she said. "It doesn't take extremely good news to be the best I've ever had." On her arm, where her brother had a self-inflicted wound, Mrs. Nissim bore her death camp number in a faint blue tattoo.

"This is extremely good news," I said. "Someone you thought was long since dead is alive."

She stood quickly, squinting at me. "Tell me it's Kurt," she said. "Please tell me it's Kurt!"

Her husband let his newspaper drop into his lap, and her daughter returned from the kitchen.

"It's Kurt," I said.

"Where is he?"

"I can arrange for you to see him soon, but I'm concerned that you are calm and can take the shock of seeing him after all these years."

"This is too good to be true! I've felt it in my heart for as long as I can remember; even when I saw in the listings at Yad Vashem that he was assumed dead, I didn't think so. I knew from people in Leipzig that he had come back to our place for some personal effects before fleeing underground. I just couldn't imagine that he would have let himself be caught again after escaping." She sat back down and looked troubled. "You know, Kurt saw more than any of the rest of us. He saw many, many people die. He was tortured. Is he all right? Has he come through this all right? Oh, I have so many questions. You said he lives in the States. When can I see him?"

"If you will compose yourself, I'll bring him in," I said. But she would have none of that. She followed me out the door and her portly middle-aged body passed me when Kurt emerged from the car. She hesitated at the sight of a face altered by years and surgery, but then he said her name in dialect as he must have as a child. Their tearful embrace moved me like nothing I had ever seen. Her husband and daughter came slowly across the street. The driver got out, and the four of us stood by the car, surrounded the curious-looking couple, and silently wept.

Epilogue

I left Kurt Burghoff in Haifa with his sister and returned to Jerusalem, where I arranged for his belongings to be sent to him. Allyson wanted to see him, but I had not even told him she was in the country. "I don't think he could take it right now. Why don't you and your mother prepare to welcome him back to Chicago when he comes," I suggested. "I think some things may change in your lives, even after all these years."

A cable waiting for me at the airport in Tel Aviv the next morning informed me that even Margo's case had turned out the opposite of what we had expected. The teacher she had suspected of being a pusher was herself an undercover police officer!

On the flight back to New York, I boldly put my arm around Allyson and held her as we talked excitedly about her plans to rebuild relationships between her father and mother and herself. "I've become very fond of you," I said.

"And I of you." She let her head drop to my shoulder. "But I'm scared."

"Of me?"

"Sort of."

"Why?"

"Because I'm falling in love with you. And the last time I did that I got hurt."

"Bad?"

"Um-hm."

"Wanna tell me about it?"

"No, but I owe it to you, because it could get in our way. I was engaged."

I stiffened.

"I loved the guy and wanted to marry him. He felt the same. There was no problem. In fact, that *was* the problem. It was too perfect. It worried me. I had never been really serious about anyone before, and now I was ready to commit myself to someone for life."

"Yeah? So what happened?"

"I asked for some time. That's all. Just some time."

"Did you get it?" I asked, barely able to get the words out.

"I'm still serving it. When I needed time, he didn't have it to give. He was married to someone else within six months."

I was speechless.

"Are you all right, Philip? Does it bother you that I was engaged?"

I shook my head.

"There was nothing about me he didn't like, he told me. He just couldn't handle it when I asked for a little time. She came along at just the right moment, and that was that. She got him."

"Are you sorry?" I managed.

"Not really. That said so much about his character that I would have hated to learn the hard way, after we were married. What if I had asked for some consideration then? It wasn't in him to allow that."

I pulled my arm back and sat staring out the window into the morning sun.

When I didn't speak for several minutes, Allyson touched my arm. "What is it, Philip?"

"I need to talk to you about something very important," I said. "Will you bear with me?"

"Of course."

"You said you were *falling* in love with me."

"Yes."

"But you haven't fallen, have you?"

"I hardly know you, Philip."

"Right. Good. Because what I'm about to tell you will help you get to know me. And then I'm afraid our relationship will have to change."

Telling her about Margo made for a painful trip home. I realized what I had done to both women. Allyson forgave me, but her tears hurt me deeply. It was my own fault. With her phrase "There was nothing about me he didn't like" ringing in my ears, I knew I had no reason to dump Margo. It wasn't just that there wasn't anything about her I didn't like. I loved her. I had loved her from early in our friendship. And I would always love her.

"She needs to know that," Allyson said. "You and she will grow from this, you know."

"I wish you and I could always be close," I said. "You'd like Margo, too."

"You know that would never work," she said, still fighting tears, as I was.

"Yeah, I do. But do me a favor, will you? Never forget that I admire you and appreciate you. You are a beautiful person."

"Thank you, Philip," she said. And she laid her head back on the tiny pillow and closed her eyes.

In Margo Mystery No. 6, *Erin*, Linda Gibbons's boyfriend, Johnny Bizell, is found murdered. Among the suspects are Greg Gibbons, Linda, Bonnie, thirteen-year-old Erin, and an unidentified maintenance man who once barged in on Linda and Johnny but who does not fit the description of anyone working in the apartment building.